Dream Traveler

Written and Illustrated by
Michele Twomey

 **New Generation Publishing**

To Chloe and Gabrielle
Your intelligence, wit, charm and beauty is the
inspiration
for not only this story but for every day of my life.

Chapter 1

I open my eyes, awakened by the roar of the engines beneath. My neck is sore from the angle my body has contorted itself, while trying to catch some sleep. This is the most bizarre feeling; it is the middle of the night for me, yet the sun begins to peek through the window. Our jumbo jet divides the clouds, giving us a glimpse of a carpet of green below. My mother is waking from sleep next to me, "Look you can almost see the countryside; it really is forty shades of green." She exclaims. I take this opportunity to shoot her a disgusted look before I roll away and pull the scratchy green blanket over my shoulders. I can hear her voice droning on asking another passenger if this is their first visit to Ireland.

Drifting back to the events of the last year, I realize I was happy enough. Ending middle school was trying. It had its moments and I almost enjoyed it. My Dad had a steady job he had been working at since I can remember. My mother's sole purpose, since I had known her was to take care of my dad and me. That was before I was introduced to those terms, that have become such a part of my life: words like "down-sizing" and "budgeting"; words I had never heard before that became all too familiar around my house.

First the long-term plans got shelved. The drawings and brochures for a backyard swimming pool inadvertently stopped lying around the family room and kitchen counters. When I asked my Mom what was up with the pool plans, she would blow me off. I knew it meant I would be spending another sweltering hot summer in the North Carolina heat, listening to the neighbors having a blast in their cool beautiful pool. I was the only thirteen going on fourteen year old in a ten-mile radius who didn't have a pool. My only consolation was that we still had our gym membership. I could always swim at that skanky pool; my mother was so quick to remind me.

The only problem with that is the thousands of other people who have the same plan. The last few times I was there, we were pulled out for various sordid misfortunes. Like the time the little kid's diaper exploded and brown sludge oozed out into the water not ten feet from where I swam. Or the time the old timer fell off the noodle he constantly bobbed around on, and cracked his head on the side, sending a red blood bath into the deep end. The list went on and on, always something would happen when I just got into the water. The whistle would blow and the teenage lifeguard would slowly climb down the set of stairs that kept him perched high enough to see the entire Olympic size pool. He would cup his hands and unceremoniously yell, "pool is closed." When I ask how long, he would shrug his shoulders, "how ever long it takes to clear this through the filters." Which usually took anywhere from two to three hours.

Then the rainy day Saturdays at the mall, slipped away. My mother and I would love to spend a lazy day rummaging the malls, I never thought about what something cost. That dwindled and before I knew it we were scouring the racks of the discount outlets, for my back to school stuff, if that wasn't bad enough my mother would constantly be asking, "if I really needed that." Then the shopping came to a complete stop.

The real tip off for me was the adoption plans. My parents had been thinking about possibly adopting a baby or even a toddler. Mom was really into it. I personally watched her spend hours researching; exhausting every possible lead. I knew she had spent countless more time when I was at school, checking foreign consulates. She was looking in to the prospect of adopting a baby from China, or Russia. She was getting pretty serious and I know she was really excited, and felt like she was closing in. That conversation just abruptly ended. No more adoption, no more foreign embassies leaving e-mails, no more anything, end of story.

My father smiled less and less when he came home from work. He talked to my mother in quiet discussions, almost whispers. When I walked into the room they would stop, and try to put on a happy face, but I wasn't stupid. I am almost fourteen - I knew something was up. Then it just stopped, the coming home from work, the work at all I should say; no more steady job and no more steady paycheck.

Next came the "temporary layoff". I think that was how he put it but I knew the truth. He was fired. My dad had lost his job. Things looked really bleak for a while. He explained, "Audrey, these are hard times." Now I wasn't worried about whether I would be taking the spring horse riding camp. I was worried about what happens next. Much more serious stuff, and the laughs and easygoing vibe in the house seemed to go with his job. Now he sat at the table hunched over his computer with his eyebrows crunched and a look of panic across his face. I don't know if there is anything more scary than seeing the man you look up to most in the world, looking terrified, and not being able to have any control over it. Who would ever think, that such a simple thing as getting by could be so frightening? Something I took for granted, having an income to support our lifestyle. Now to see my dad, the one I counted on to continually chase the boogey-man from under my bed- the man who rode in on his magical steed, a pink stuffed horse head mounted on a stick. Galloping in to save me from my imprisonment in the dank dungeons, otherwise known as the family room ottoman. Scooping me in

7

one arm while my polyester princess gown flowed freely. This man was my hero, my champion, and now I saw and felt real fear as I looked into his scared and defeated eyes.

Then to add insult to injury, my mother goes off and finds work. I know we needed the money, but this seemed to make my father feel even worse. She glides in and does what he can't seem to do; she earns a paycheck. Fortunately, or unfortunately for our family budget, she could only find some part-time contractual work. She spends the occasional month of late night hours here and there, grueling hours on the computer. I spend my time watching the back of her head as she is bent over the screen, feverously punching in data, fighting some unrealistic deadline. "Free-lance contractual work" is what she called it. Barely there and never able to count on her, is what I called it. She would complete one assignment and take a few days off to catch up on sleep and be back at it again. She was obvious pretty good at what she did, because there seem to always be another task, lurking in the background, waiting to take her away.

Suddenly my father's spirit lifted, he was so excited to tell us about his "summer assignment". Great the guy will finally have something to do. I was all for it. I was happy for him, when he started to explain the details. I was thinking about my friends, and school, half listening as he rattled on. Until I realized, what he was saying. He used the words "learning experience."

Heads up, when your parents use those kind of words it means one thing: complete mindless boredom, only in my case it was even worse. My father was plotting something, and this wasn't one afternoon, this was going to be my entire summer. He wanted to pack us all up and take us to Ireland? Suddenly he had my full attention. "Uh, Dad, did you say Ireland - for the

8

whole summer? Maybe I could come over for a couple of weeks, then stay at the Dawson's?" Geez at this point I would have taken Nana coming to stay with me. Anything else, I can't be away for the entire summer. No way, this will not be happening. I had suffered enough through this awful recession, now he thought he could just yank me away from what little life I have left.

An eight week get-away to Ireland he called it. Conveniently planned over my summer break. We are to pack ourselves up, and head out to who knows where for some random work project. He explained it as a wonderful opportunity to work for an American company abroad. It's an incredible opportunity for him. For me it's a colossal disaster. I had my summer already planned, thank you very much.

"Duty Free?" The flight attendant disrupts my anger to ask if I would like to take advantage of this final chance, to buy any tax-free trinkets. She asks me something else, but my own thoughts about being dragged here are yelling over her voice. Whatever lady, am I supposed to understand Irish accents now too? This is unbelievable. I give her one of my favorite fake smiles, this particular one I have practiced for hours in the mirror. I call it my, nonchalant, with a hint of back off. It seems to work, she clanks her cart full of wares further down the aisle. Unfortunately she hasn't traveled far enough. The guy behind me gives in to his mini maniac's tantrum, the miniature version of himself, who travels in the seat next to him. He picks out a tacky green plane, with a shamrock on the side. This seems to humor, the whiny kid. Now the brat is circling it over my head, and ramming it into the seat behind me. What is particularly humiliating about this scene is that the toy is an exact replica of the plane we are presently riding on. One good thing about traveling to another country, there is no one to witness these incredibly lame moments. Finally the intrusion is over and I am given a moment to focus on myself.

I can't believe my parents are putting me through this. My first summer since finishing middle school and my father drags me here. These two people, who I once knew to be my parent's, are systematically ruining my life. "A learning adventure," I think that's the phrase Mom enjoys throwing around to describe this misadventure. I prefer to describe it as the demise of my social life. This can't be happening. I look over at my mother; she can't possibly be buying into this craziness. She looks tired and her pretty blue eyes seem to have grayed. There are tiny lines forming around her mouth. I think this whole job stuff has really aged her. Her once healthy blond hair now looks dull and faded. She has let it grow out and it seems to lengthen her face more, giving her a skeletal look. Luckily, being so tired allows me a short surrender to sleep as our plane taxis to the gate.

Waiting at the baggage carousel, watching the bags circle, I spot my purple and fuchsia striped bag. Reaching down my blood begins to boil as I notice the bright neon sticker plastered to the side, it is a U.S. customs tag. It states in bold print that as a security precaution my luggage was searched. Great, some complete stranger has riffled through my bag. I have been completely violated. My father's response to this gross intrusion is, "suck it up Audrey." I glare at him before replying through gritted teeth; "I don't even know you anymore." I am cursing at his back as he collects our luggage. I make sure to point out how comforted he must feel knowing his worldly possessions weren't ransacked by strangers. A tiny smile forms at his lip as we make for the corridor leading to the terminals.

Finally the stairs, which lead out of this stuffy basement that someone has loosely called baggage claim. We travel through a hall of mirrors. I am mortified at the reflection staring back at me. "Uggh" I gasp. We boarded a plane last night at 10pm. Six hours later, I am standing in a hallway of mirrors, in this strange country, a room full of custom agents most likely staring back at me from behind the glass. I am sure they are having a great laugh at the sight of what is left of my hairstyle.

Yesterday, which now seems a lifetime ago, I carefully brushed out my thick brown hair, and let some of the body remain. No easy task, since I have decided to let it grow out. My hair is thick, and unruly when left to its own devices. I carefully blow - dried and spritzed the mass, leaving only a few of the many curls, which pop out in deformed clusters at the first sign of humidity. I had immediately noticed the lack of moisture in the plane's cabin, so I felt confident that I wouldn't be faced with any frizzy issues. I am shocked to see that I am suffering a far greater fate. One side of my hair is completely smashed, plastered to my skull. This gives new meaning to the word "bed-head". I look like I haven't slept at all. It is hard to see that my eyes are blue, they are rimmed red and bloodshot, it looks like some sort of neon red eyeliner. I keep my head down as we pass through the last security checkpoint and head out into the main terminal.

Waiting on the black plastic couches, while my father secures a rental car gives me the first opportunity to dig through my carry on bag. I run my hands through the mess of all familiar belongings, my only comfort in this strange place. I feel the familiar finish of my phone, the sleek smooth metal almost cool to the touch. With a slow comfortable pleasure I rub my fingers over it as I bring the slick surface to my cheek.

"What time is it in North Carolina?" I ask my mother. "Oh man, it is completely dead. I forgot to charge it before we left." I half scream back at her. Mom looks as if she may say something, but after hearing my tone she changes her mind.

I dig deeper into the bag to pull out my instant hair do. Aha there it is, my favorite canvas patchwork hat. The beauty of this cap is no matter how wrinkled and worn it gets the better it seems to look. If my hair was a bucking bronco, then this simple canvas hat would be "the horse whisperer." Tossing it on, my head instantly combats all the massive frizz and kink. Wrangling it in to quiet submission. A quick reshape and I throw it on my head to work its magic, as we head outside to my father in the waiting car.

As soon as the terminal doors open and we step out I feel it. It is the freshest air, clear and clean it covers me. I take in a quick breath. The next step with the second breath is a mix of diesel fuel and exhaust. The terminal entrance road is alive with huge tour buses and tiny cars of strange makes and models, buzzing pass on the wrong side of the road, all pushing to load and unload passengers. We transfer our stuff into the foreign rental car, and hop in. It is one thing to see the cars driving on the other side of the road, but to actually be inside one with the driver on the passenger side is another kind of weird. "It is going to be a long drive, so get comfortable sweetie." Mom says in a raspy voice, her eyelids are red and puffy. Her voice barely audible mumbling in the far distance, as I give in once again to the sleep that follows me like a shadow.

Chapter 2

I am not sure if I slept for minutes or hours, it is amazing how tired my body feels. Finally, I pull myself awake. I can't believe the traffic flow around here. We are off the main road and onto a series of strips of concrete with green in the center. This can't be a two-lane road. It is so narrow that my dad must pull off into the hedges in order to let a car pass. The car has brambles and vines stuck to the side view mirror. Showing me where he has clipped the hedges, while I slept.

"Are they calling this two lanes," I ask. My eyes focus from what feels to be a restless nap. We are now on a series of tiny roads that wind around the many huge fields. Up and down hills and inclines, it's a massive tangle of different roads; again I use the term "road" loosely. They look far more like glorified walking paths. On the rare occasion that we face another car, one must chose to pull into the grassy patch on the side and stop. The driver that passes first gives a nod and moves on. The countryside can be spotted in little glimpses over the hedges or at the top of a hill. As far as the eye can see lays endless fields. A brambly hedge or small rock wall maps out designated pastures, a medley of different shades of emerald. All framed by a hodge-podge collection of pastures. Rocks dot the fields here and there. There is a real sense of tranquil peace in this vast collection of green.

We pull into a narrow driveway made up of small stones, the car crunches along till we stop in front of a white plaster house. It is built into the side of a hill. There is an embankment on the left- dotted with orange flowers; the top opens to a field of weeds and wildflowers. Everywhere you look is green and lush with hardy flowers boasting multiple blooms. Bringing the luggage up a few steps allows a view of a massive pasture that borders the property on the other side. The sky is magnificent, the shade of perfectly faded jeans. A set of colossal clouds shoots off masses of white puffy orbs that are weighted with grayish blue bottoms. Each gracefully glide over my head within a matter of seconds. Multiplying to cover us with a cool shadow. A wooden deck surrounds the front of the house on this level; it widens at the front stoop and then thins as it winds around the side. Before my father can finish turning the key in the front door, I feel a raindrop hit me in the back. The heavy wood door lets out a small squeak, as we push the last of our belongings in before the downpour. It is sort of charming, in a foreign strange way. A tile entryway opens above to a banister with light wood rails, holding in a small office, on the floor overhead. The rain has changed into a downpour pounding the twin skylights that lay next to each other on walls sloping to form the upstairs office ceiling. A dark shadow casts gray where moments before floods of light sent in a warm glow. The house is on multiple levels with short staircases that lead to different landings. I am anxious to explore but my body feels so heavy. I am not sure what time it is here or back home, but I am starved. We make our way towards the back of the house. Every room is behind a door. It seems odd to me, a sharp contrast to our house where every room is open with high ceilings.

A beautiful bouquet of flowers on the island welcomes us into the country kitchen. Everything is behind pale yellow clapboard cupboards; one reveals the dishwasher, and one hides a refrigerator of sorts. This one is a quarter the size of our fridge. Amazingly enough the miniature version of a fridge holds quite a bit of food. "Oh that Deidre is so thoughtful, come and look Jack." My mom says. I lug my carry on canvas bag onto the kitchen table and begin searching for my electronics and their various cords.

"Where should I plug my phone into Dad?" I ask. "Listen Audrey" he stutters as he seems to be planning out his words. He answers awkwardly. "The electrical outlets are different, and we sort of forgot to sign you up for an international calling plan," he gives me a meek half smile. "What, are you telling me I have no link to the outside world?" My reply sounds more like a shrill then a question. "You can use my computer to e-mail your friends, we can set up some sort of adaptor, and I will look into an international plan," he pleads. "E-MAIL, please, nobody e-mails anymore, and from a stationery unit, Ugghhh this is barbaric".

I am furious. I storm out of the kitchen and loudly push through the pocket wood doors. I find myself in a sunroom. There is only a piano in the odd shaped room, completely surrounded by windows. Through the thick glass I see the wood decking which widens to a large rectangle on this side of the house. It is a set up for outside dining with an umbrella table and odd benches and chairs. Each seat offers the chance to take advantage of the stellar views of the expansive countryside beyond. I follow the lamp cord, noticing the chunky European electric plug. "Unbelievable." I whisper as the rain begins to slow lifting the mist. I can see an old barn farther up the hill.

A small dark shape moves across the massive field. The figure is slight and small like that of a kid. I watch it as it covers the field, leaps the fence and now moves into the back yard. I reluctantly open the door. A round faced girl, of around eight, wearing a dark raincoat and huge rubber boots appears before me. She looks pale, and kind of pasty; sort of the color of glue that sticks to the edge of the stick too long. She pulls off the hood from her thick raincoat. Water sprays out and falls onto the tile floor. A tangle of strawberry blond tight curls fall to her shoulders followed by more droplets of water. "Hi, I am Anna" she says with complete confidence. I give her a slow once over. Starting my glare at the top of her head and slowly moving over her entirely. I squint my eyes at the mess of water she has pooling at her feet. She follows my gaze and smiles before starting again, " My Ma wanted to make sure you are getting settled in properly." Her accent is thick, but I can still understand most of what she is saying. "What did you say your name was, Alana?" I ask maybe a little sarcastically, trying to look intimidating. Her light brown eyes show just a slight flicker of hurt as she nods, "No Anna Byrne, my Ma is Deidre." "Oh come in," my mother chimes in over me, "I am Kelly Peters and this is my husband Jack, and this is Audrey. Please tell your Mom we love the place, and come in and join us for some breakfast, please." "Way to sound desperate Mom," I say under my breath. My Mom doesn't seem to hear me but I notice Anna looks straight at me, with those honey colored eyes. I follow her into the kitchen watching her wispy blond curls bounce with each step.

The smell from the kitchen reaches me as I turn away from her questioning stare. I had forgotten how hungry I am, ahead lays a bounty of bacon, eggs and sausage. " Lovely," she says quickly peeling off her wet coat and boots. She shows my mother where the plates and silverware are. She is very much at ease in the large country kitchen. Everyone starts filling up plates as we huddle around the kitchen island. I look over at my useless phone cord dangling out of my bag, with its slim plug. My anger begins to rise. I am reminded again of the situation, the predicament I have been put in, the burden and inconvenience. I glare at my parents, how can they just sit there and eat? Look at what I have been put through. I look towards the happy three-some, enjoying their food in this strange place, no one even caring about me.

Giving a snide smile as I turn to the group, "Anna, you seem awfully young, to be out alone, do your parents always let you just wander around these fields?" I can see the embarrassment rise and flush across my mother's cheeks, even before I finish the question. "It is funny you should ask that, young lady." This time my father answers, the vein on the top of his forehead bulges when he is angry, and now it is almost like it has a separate pulse. I am so busy starring at it I hardly notice the disappointment in his tone, "We have agreed that this summer you will be helping out by keeping an eye on Anna during the week." Staring at me, his eyes darkening. He knows I won't let this go without a fight. He removes his glasses and runs his hands through his hair.

My father is not a large man, or a loud one; he looks more the bookworm brainy type. He wins arguments with his silence, and his ability to remain unemotional.

I glare deep into his green eyes. "What, you drag me half away around the world and now you are making me work? I believe there are trafficking laws, and child labor laws being violated here." I have been in enough disagreements with my dad to know, he is looking for weakness. I roll my shoulders back, a clear message to him that I am not backing down.

Leaning back, he takes a moment to digest my outburst. He looks me straight in the eye, his voice controlled, "You will be accompanying our friend Anna, while we stay."

The battle is over now, but the war will continue. We retreat to our corners temporarily.

I finally settle on a bedroom, the cool one at the top of all the stairs apart from all the others. It is past the office, through a door that is surrounded by bookshelves. The room is a powder blue color with a slanted ceiling that follows the roofline. It has two skylights that are perpendicular, each with a pale pink shade. The closet doors are also slanted, and inside there is plenty of room. After wrestling my clothes on to the hangers, I fall on the soft bed with the pale pink comforter. This house is so comfortable; it is set up for a family, except where are the personal possessions? I wonder about this house's backstory, as I drift off to sleep.

Chapter 3

The rain on the skylight wakes me as I drag myself out of heavy sleep. A rush of panic, hits square in the chest. I haven't spoken to any one in almost three days. I race down the stairs and into the kitchen, nearly knocking my mother down where she stands making a list of groceries. "Where's Dad, where's the laptop?" I scream.

"Well good morning," my mother answers before being interrupted by the doorbell. The upper half of the front door is all glass, so I recognize the figure. "It's that girl," I say as I look for the case that carries the laptop, my only source to the outside world. I realize its nowhere in sight; it must be with my Dad. I can hear my mother's voice as I try to skirt past. "Come in Anna." Looking over them and out the window, my heart drops as I see the empty spot, where the rental car was parked. He must have gone into work with it. I am going to have to set up some kind of schedule with him. I can't believe he would just go to his job, for an entire day, without allowing me the chance to check my e-mails. I turn away and slowly walk in the opposite direction from my mother and Anna.

Stepping into the sunroom and sharply pulling open the piano to expose the keys: I sit. I play no particular tune. This isn't helping to improve my mood. I try every annoying song I know. I smile coyly as I play some of my favorite little ditties, thinking back proudly on how these simple notes drove my piano teacher to the edge. On second thought, I guess that isn't saying much. My teacher is an incredibly wicked woman, who always seems to be on the brink of some sort of breakdown. She took great pleasure in letting her students know that she found their playing obnoxious. In fact as soon as a parent walked out of the room, her mood would darken. She would tense her back and immediately cop an attitude. It is amazing to me how so many people will treat you completely different in front of your parents, as opposed to how they treat you when they're not around them. Do they not know you can tell? Oh well, that is one thing I don't mind giving up with all this job loss crap - those awful afternoons spent playing the piano with Mrs. Flanders in her rotten smelling den.

The ground behind me lets out a thunder, distracting me from my horrible memories of piano. Turning slowly I see a group of horses, running through the fog that lingers over the massive field Anna crossed last night. I am positive it is my playing that has brought them. I don't have long to relish in the fact that I have tamed these wild beasts with my abilities, because Anna steps through the double doors carrying a bag of carrots. The horses seem to recognize her immediately. It is her they are responding to, not me. "Are these your horses?" I ask, stepping out the door behind her. "Oh no they belong to the Murphy's." As she answers a large gray that is dappled nuzzles her. "Well, they sure seem to know you." The horse lovingly grabs a carrot from her hands. She shrugs her shoulders and gives a sad nod. She makes sure each horse gets a treat. The clouds once again race across the sky, this time giving way to a sunny day beneath.

"Come on we can head into town, if you like?" She asks, her mood now noticeably brighter. "Well I need to find my Dad, but after that, okay." I reply, smiling at her. I can't help but catch one of her curls in my finger. I gently twist it around before placing it back on her petite shoulder. There is something likeable about her. Something natural and real about her, she carries no pretense. It can't hurt to give the little squirt a chance, at least she knows her way around town.

I borrow a pair of boots from the stocked closet. My mother mentions seeing us in town later, and before we head out she tosses me seven oversized European coins. Being so heavy, they put a bulge in my gabardine shorts. "Wow, thanks Mom." Making sure to lay the sarcasm on extra heavy, she can be a little slow when it comes to feeling my disappointment.

At the end of the driveway there is a thin red string across the entrance. I pull it up and step out, under protest from Anna. The road in front of our house is packed with cows. The herd crowds in the narrow road to avoid the figures walking behind. "Get back." A voice from farther up the road yells towards me. Quickly I pull back behind the string as the stinky filthy procession passes. "You are lucky you caught them heading out to graze, if you stepped out on the road on their way home, you might have been trampled." The farmer says in a patronizing tone. "Oh, Anna, I didn't see you there luv." This time the farmer's voice takes on a softer tone as he asks, "How are ya, my little darling?" "Fine, thanks Mr. Kennedy, and how are you this morning?" she responds. The rest of the Kennedy's bid good morning as they pass, swinging their sticks to keep the herd in line. "A real family affair" I say as an older man leads, followed by a man who is a clone of him only twenty or thirty years younger. Behind him a woman and two small children. All with shabby mud splattered clothes. The children's sweaters are stretched out and everyone carries a layer of grimy dirt on them. They each bring their own stick occasionally swinging it up in the air. The stick acts as a constant reminder to the cows to remain in line.

"That's right Audrey, everyone in the family helps out when it comes to tending the herd. The Kennedy's fields need resting so they are renting pasture space from the Murphy's down the road. You better get use to keeping an eye out. They will be passing by every morning bringing the herd out to graze and everyday around half four they pass back with the cows full of milk, and hunger. He is right about not wanting to step out in front of them, they want to get home and eat their dinner, and unload their milk." She answers knowingly; amused by the way I crinkle my nose. "Wow, they really stink up the place, don't they?" I ask. "Well it could be where you're standing," she says with a giggle. I look down to see my boot is up to the ankle in cow patties."

"GROSS." I scream, taking multiple scrapes on the old stonewall to remove all the cow crap collecting on my rubber boots. Finally the last bit of muck oozes off my boot and hits the road with a slap. The family is laughing as they continue down the windy road. "I am glad I can bring you all such joy." I quip curtly. It is hard to be angry with Anna, she has a contagious giggle, and I end up joining in. "What is up with half four?" I ask, trying to distance myself from the cow incident. "Does half four mean four thirty?" She quickens her step to catch me with a questioning look on her face, "I think so?" she responds.

The smallest Kennedy darts in front of us, he runs back to collect the thin red yarn, rolling into a ball in his tiny hands. As we continue down the road, I think about that little guy spending the day running ahead at every opening or driveway. He rigs the yarn so that the cows will stay on track, then doubles back after to collect it all over again. He is having a great time and it is obvious he truly enjoys his work. His dirty face carries a proud smile under scarlet cheeks. A slight trail of wetness runs from his nose leaving a clean path of pale skin. The rest of his face covered in dirt and mud. A reminder of places he has been so far.

We climb the last hill, below is the village. Ancient stone buildings line the winding, thin cobblestone roads. Some of the old stores have been painted in bright colors, windows cleaned and shiny. It looks like a lame attempt to hide the fact that the village is hundreds of years old. Other buildings look as if they have remained the same for centuries. I can make out a small grocery store, a pub, and a fish shop. A bank in fresh salmon colored tones stands at the corner. Every building that faces the town square is painted in bright colors and newly washed. With flowerpots out front, all in different hues, the front sidewalks are neatly swept. Winding around the outside of the town center a small basin that acts as the village harbor. The harbor leads to a twisting channel of water that leads to a wider channel and out to the open sea.

Before we enter the village we stop on an incredible footbridge. Sitting on the large stonewalls that make up just one of the many sides. The beauty of this medieval overpass leaves me in awe. The edges have been smoothed from the elements battering them for years. I can tell each stone was hammered and chiseled by hand, made to fit tightly together long before cement ever was around.

Dangling our feet over the edge, our boots just barely touch the blue green water below. The cove is so quiet, the water so calm. Temporary metal piers have been quickly installed, a slight reminder of what century we are in. Based on all the docking space I would say this little village has a lot of water traffic. Most docks are littered with metal cleats, flat metal bolts with horns on each side, waiting for boats to secure their numerous ropes assuring the vessels safety while docking. In the belly of the inlet old fishing boats and cabin cruisers are moored to bright colored buoys. Bobbing and weaving, many more buoy lay vacant, in all different directions and all kinds of sizes, they bob and sway with the breeze. "Why are there so many places to dock," I ask. "Oh, soon the summer tourists will be everywhere, the harbor gets so crowded it's a wonder there aren't more accidents. Captain McMahon, the harbor captain is still out to sea fishing. When he comes back he will sort it out." I can see out past the inlet and into the far rocky channel, vessels of varying sizes troll slowly back and forth on the large waves that dot the horizon.

"How long do, the fishing boats go out to sea for?" I ask. Anna mumbles something about anywhere from a week to three months. Her eyes suddenly turn sad, and fill with tears. Momentarily at a loss for words, I struggle to say something - anything. "Are you okay?" Is all I am able to get out. She brushes past me, an obvious attempt to blow off my question, she bends to pick up a small stone from the cobblestone road and throws it off the opposite side of the bridge in an effort to turn her back to me. Okay, this seems pretty big, whatever has her this upset. I will let go of it and not question her, at least for now, anyway.

I glance into the blue green water and see my reflection on the calm sea. It is so still, it's as if I am looking into a mirror. I am admiring my hair when something slices through the center of my image. My face in the water breaks. A number of long ripples escape. A flash of silver or gray glimmers for only an instant, then it is gone. It is far too large and agile to be a fish. It vanishes again, as quickly as it appears. In the blue depths, a splash catches me off guard, soaking my face with cold seawater. I look again to the source of the assault, but the water is just a puddle of ripples. I trail behind Anna, licking the sea salt from my lips as I study the water.

We meet up with my mother and grab lunch at one of the many cafes that line the sea. It allows me the perfect view of the harbor and some of the locals. Leading me to partake in one of my favorite past times, people watching. Starting out with someone's shoes, I move up from there. The diverse selection of foot ware has been amazing since landing in this strange country. It makes for some interesting people watching. Faces look the same but the clothing and shoes are so different. The men and boys wear jerseys with team logos or sponsors. But weird ones that I have never heard of before. The other thing is, no one but children wear tennis shoes. No runners, or sneakers. All the men wear the same shoes my Dad wears to work, dress loafers with jeans. The woman and even young girls all opt for boots, with or without heels or loafers. Only the young children wear anything even close to resembling gym shoes.

My mother and Anna chat away through lunch about subjects I have no interest in. My mind keeps returning to the water and the "alien creature incident." The silver thing that shot through my reflection, there is no way that thing was a fish. "Have you ever seen any creatures in the sea," I casually ask Anna. "What kind of creatures," her response shows a hint of amusement, she seems to guard her answer as if I may be baiting her. I can tell she doesn't take the conversation very seriously. I squint my eyes in anger. "Oh forget it," I sigh, making sure to convey resentment over her sarcasm. There is no way I am going to trust some eight year old kid. Especially one I am stuck hand holding all summer. She is just lucky she had that little breakdown out on the bridge, other wise I would be letting her have it.

I don't usually let someone make me feel stupid. Not without verbally tearing them apart a little. I think I might be getting a little soft, between that and the whole "sea monster" thing. I must be suffering some serious long-term jet lag. The more I think about it the more I think it may have been a big fish, or a shadow.

After lunch we walk back to the house, Anna disappears across the field. The same way she appeared on that first day. Another day I will be anxious to see where exactly she goes, and what exactly is her scoop.

For now, I have my own pressing business. Finally, I am able to get a hold of Dad's laptop. When I first mentioned to my friends that I would be gone for the entire summer, I felt a chill, a distance. Part of the obligation of being in a "popular" group in middle school is that you remain available. You have to answer a majority of your texts, maintain a social network site, or in my case since my parents didn't let me have one, be in most of the photos and stories on someone else's page. I worked hard to gain the social status I sort of enjoyed. I had to endure countless remarks - without even the slightest look of hurt-from "my dearest friends." Somehow in the last year it became popular in my group to say something hurtful and mean, to sort of lash out at someone who is suppose to be your friend. You can say anything you want, as long as you end with those two magic words "just kidding." It is sort of a rite of passage, to see if you can stand completely unaffected by someone else words. No matter how much they hurt.

My heart pounds loudly as the system finally boots up. With shaky hands I punch in my password. "You have no new messages from contacts" greets me. I sit back in the tall chair, and wait for another line of copy to spell out " just kidding." It doesn't come, so I safely let down my guard. A few tears spill down my cheeks at first, and then, I cry. A cry that has been deep inside me, one I pushed back until it couldn't stay down anymore. I do go out of my way to make sure my parents don't hear me in the other room. The green cast from off the computer fades to black, I wipe the last of my tears away as I close the cover.

Chapter 4

The first sound I hear from my room upstairs is the doorbell, quickly followed by voices. My mother is greeting Anna like they have known each other for years. "Whatever Mom," I blurt aloud. Why is this kid constantly over here? Doesn't she have a home of her own?

My mother is busy peddling out my services as babysitter and bodyguard. She interrupts her own talking to call me down. "I am coming." I snap.

Anna's mother comes into view first. A tall woman of around thirty-five, her strong resemblance to Anna proves me right. They have the same tight curls and stocky figure. She is somehow connected to the company my dad is working for, or wants to be working for, so I know I can't be too rude. I turn on the stairs, with a half smile. "Hello Audrey, I am Deidre, what a pleasure it is to meet you. What a luv you are, to help us out this summer with Anna. I hope it won't be too much of a bother for you dear."

Deidre rambles on about how grateful she is due to the circumstances and all, blah, blah, blah. She goes on for a bit longer. I am only half listening. I smile graciously, all the while thinking of the predicament I am in. I have been taken from my homeland, and now I am being used to chaperone some kid around town. There are sweatshops in third world countries that pay better for their child labor, than what I am getting. Which so far has amounted to no more than a few euro coins to spend at some out dated shop.

"Come on Audrey, I want to show you something, in for a walk?" Anna chimes in. She already knows me well enough at this point to I see I don't listen to adults drone on with their pleasantries.

My father is heading in the drive, and my mother and Deidre are setting on a pot of tea. Weighing my options, I decide taking a hike, must be more fun than hanging around here. I pull the old rubber boots on, the faint remains of the cow waste barely visible. Straightening out my canvas hat and tossing it over my ever-expanding hair, I give Anna a nod and we are off.

This time we head behind the house and up the narrow road towards the forest. The day has changed again. Now a rain blasts across the road in front of us. I am glad I chose my hat because this is the kind of humidity that sends my hair into a frizz patch, resembling some sort of nest.

The rain is more of a misty drizzle, then a downpour. Just like when you turn the hose nozzle on to the "mist" mode. It looks strong and blustery, a real soaker, but when under it, you barely get wet. Oh well, it's a hair frizzier all the same. I raise my hand to see if I can collect any of the rain, it doesn't quite materialize; it just vaporizes into a moist air.

"If you don't like this weather, just wait a moment, you will get another option soon enough." Anna says, waiting to see if I like the joke. "Forget your raincoat, no worries; the sun will be along in a jiffy." Her voice a little winded. She is right; the weather here changes every hour or two. I don't know how any one would plan an outside event. The road becomes considerably steeper, and I work harder, a slight burning in my calves. We climb higher still, straight up for what seems like an eternity. The shadows from the forest trees continue to grow longer as the afternoon gets older.

She abruptly turns and squeezes through a hole in the hedge. It opens to a patch of thick green grass. From there, she skirts between two large pines and disappears in the darkness. I have to jog to try to keep up with her. She seems to disappear and reappear at the drop of a hat. I really hate when she does that.

Entering the darkness, the cool air cascades over me; the scent of wet pine is refreshingly sweet and a carpet of pine needles, soft and slippery pile under my boots. The forest lets me out of its grip and drops me into a wide field where grass grows as high as my waist.

I trip on huge stone boulders littered everywhere in all shades of brown. Small structures and towers seem to grow out of the ground. Gradually, I realize I am looking at some kind of ancient building ruins.

I feel a warm breath on my shoulder, "Anna, you scared the crap out of me." I whip myself around. Eye to eye, I meet the gaze of a cow. She bends down and grabs a clump of the long grass at my feet. Yanking it out of the ground with ease she begins chewing it loudly, watching me while, light green spittle forms and trickles out the sides of her mouth. "You are absolutely disgusting, shouldn't you be tied to something," I say in a soft lilting voice, as another one wanders up. "Oh, how nice, you brought your skivvy fat friends, and you too have rotten yellow teeth. Lovely, if you will excuse me, I am just passing through."

Gradually I back away from the small cluster of cows that are beginning to form. Everywhere I look, I see cows, maneuvering between the castle ruins, completely oblivious to me, they walk around in an almost zombie like state. I have never been alone in the open with cattle and I am finding it kind of unnerving. "I guess all this grass leads to a healthy digestive system," I remark, trying not to convey my nervousness in front of the herd, while dodging various degrees of decaying cow poop piles at the same time. "ANNA" my voice more of a scream, "Where the heck are you?"

After a few steps, my nervousness gives way to absolute awe. I have forgotten about the cow manure and step blindly through piles of it. The ruins upon closer inspection appear to be some kind of castle.

Luckily I had Miss Perkins for medieval studies last semester, her passion for the subject was contagious. Her knowledge about the old architecture adds the insight I need to piece the massive place back together in my mind. It must have been a huge structure or structures. Rooms and walls seem to go on for a good acre. Some of the chambers still contain the outline of the stone with remnants of a kitchen hearth, or a fireplace, clearly visible. There is a center courtyard and tiny annex. Some walls are kind of intact, and extend two to three stories high, displaying rectangle holes cut and trimmed out to form windows.

I enter an area that looks like it may have been a kitchen for either nobles or some large important group, compared to some of the smaller rooms. This place was definitely used to accommodate some serious crowds.

The skeleton remains of a huge fireplace take up the entire length of the wall. The other side yields a small grassy knoll where a low stonewall partially left, marks out an enclosure. A small enclave that was sheltered from the weather elements. I can imagine things got pretty windy up here. It probably once held a garden, the food cupboard for the massive kitchen perhaps a place where the fruit trees and vegetable gardens would have grown sheltered and safe. It is about the size of my backyard, so I imagine it would have held a lot of crops, remnants of the stonewall that once protected the garden are dotted all around the perimeters.

The whole place must at one time or other used an incredible amount of stone for its construction. It makes you wonder, who dragged all this stone up here? How did they ever get those stones to connect and stay together for so many centuries? It is hard to believe I am standing where a thousand years earlier a bustling community most likely thrived. This is something out of "The Knights of the Roundtable."

A part of me, feels so fortunate to be experiencing this, I love this stuff. I climb a tiny knoll, to take in the view. The castle once stood on what appears to be the highest point in the land. To the right, far below is the village, a tiny spot almost completely enclosed by sea. The cars moving like toys back and forth over the bridges. The buildings are no bigger than my pinky finger. I can see from this high vantage point that at some time, someone has built an incredible complex system of stone canals. It would have been an amazing feat to do now with all the building equipment we have today. I can't imagine how you would do it with no tools or tractors. It is mind blowing.

My history teacher would be freaking out if she could see this. The twisted tangle of man made channels wind and tame the sea as it slows and manages the water as best it can. Once it is close in to the village towards the inlet, the antique dyke tries it best in its primitive, but effective fashion to rein in the mighty deep. A demanding task for the ancient stone walls that border the tiny cobblestone streets. A last restraint as the wall curves one last time, allowing the water to finally rest in the swollen belly shaped harbor.

To my left, I watch the clouds roll out to the vast and wide opening of blues that is the Irish Sea. I understand why the village has tried so hard to discipline and tame this powerful water. It is an amazing swirling blend of blue and green, with commanding waves that produce raging swells. Each wave wears a massive white cap. Even from this high up I can see how the ocean is sheer power and force. Huge stone boulders poke out from the middle of the water. The ocean smashes the water onto the rocks, spraying and hissing the over spill back into the volatile water below.

Every direction has a spectacular view. "Amazing," I whisper the only term that comes into my head. The path continues winding around out-crops, virtually hanging above the perilous cliffs below. I am considering whether I should double back or proceed on ahead. The chewing sound greets me once again. I hear the slow methodical hooves, with the warm stale putrid breath on my neck. I speak directly to my buddy the bovine, "Quite a view you have here. All day you get to hang out in ancient castles, and check out the ocean." The cows begin to follow me, as if they are actually listening to me. "Some life you and your girlfriends, have. Surrounded by these ocean views, back in the states where I come from; there is no way this land would be left to a bunch of cows. Some builder or developer would have built mega mansions, a gated community to keep out the riff-raff, like you and me."

The realization that I am talking to a cow quiets me. Great I am not only talking to; but I am actually kind of relating to cows now. Shaking my head in dismay I lift my boots high to wade through the tall grass. I continue my conversation with the group, "Look, it has been great getting to know you and the girls, but I really need to find my friend, she walks on two feet. Later ladies."

Following the remains of the castle wall, leads to another whole courtyard, with still another vantage point of what once must have been a massive structure, this place must have rocked in its day.

It is easy to get side tracked off the paths, lost in the glorious views. At least the paths are buffered by patches of green, which add some consolation that there might be time to catch myself before tumbling down to the rocky cliffs below.

Before I imagine too many deadly accident scenarios I catch sight of Anna sitting on a path. Running to her, I clutch her arm, a poor attempt to keep her with me so as not to lose her again. I sit down next to her. "Where have you been? You just left. I had no idea, where I was... these cliffs are deadly... are you aware there are cows running loose... just milling around? Do they ever fall over the cliffs, or hurt themselves, or charge you? How about that castle, what is up with that? Do you ever trip on all the stones lying around the place?"

Prior to finishing my flood of questions, I hear laughing from the outcrop above my head. A boy of about fifteen is standing a few feet higher on the path, holding a white bucket nearly full of wild black berries. With a considerable thicker Irish accent than Anna he says," wow, Americans do talk fast!" Anna still looking at the ocean, adds, "Audrey, this is my cousin, Declan. "Pleasure is mine." I respond snidely giving him my canned phony smile. He smiles and shakes his head, unimpressed by my negative intimidation tactics. He turns back to his overgrown hedge and his berry picking. This gives me an opportunity to study him.

I am slightly intrigued. He has the same sort of lack of pretense that Anna has. He looks to have dark features, but it is hard to tell because he is tanned, sort of weathered in a way. I would say this guy spends a lot of time outside. He doesn't look much like Anna who is fair and pale, where he has dark and more chiseled features. He is her cousin, but looks nothing like Deidre.

His foreign jeans are dirty, with small holes at the knees. Accompanied with very worn and heavy looking work boots. I am amazed he is able to get around these sketchy paths in those. He is wearing the same sort of soccer jersey I have seen in town. Covered in some strange team logo, I never heard of, his outfit is splattered with a collection of stains in varying purples and blues. A sampling of some of the berries he has collected.

"Anna was just giving you a chance to take it all in. She meant you no harm." He says defensively. I am taken in by his protective tone and tender smile. It is obvious he has a close relationship with Anna. I sense a kindred spirit kind of vibe. I can relate to his affection for her, she does have a way of getting under your skin. There is more to this kid, a deeper side.

I too feel as if I want to shelter her. I take a seat next to her on the thin path and she passes a handful of blackberries towards me. Declan sits down on the other side of her and we begin to devour the remains of what he has collected in his pail.

"Some hang out you guys have here. Have you been coming here long?" I ask, digging my boot into the side of the dirt path. Declan is the first to answer, "Ya, my Uncle's place is just around the bend, these are his cows. I have been coming since I was a wee lad. Anna is new to up here."

Knowing this next statement may sound incredibly uncool; I feel the need to ask her anyway. "Isn't it a little dangerous up here for you?" She looks off at the endless horizon before answering, "I have to come, Audrey, it's the best place to watch for the fishing boats." Her voice trails off, and she retreats into that sadness again.

"I want to be here when my father comes back." Her voice begins to break and crack as she continues. "I want to be here, as soon as he clears the open sea. I need enough time to run into town and meet him at the harbor when his boat docks."

Declan puts his head down before adding. "No worries, Anna, we will all try to keep an eye out." "Ya, that's the problem everyone has an eye out. Only they keep those eyes out on me. Poor Anna. Why do you think Mum brings in some girl from halfway around the world? She finally found someone who hasn't heard the sad story of poor Anna. She has you keeping an eye on me, spying so I don't run off or go off my rocker, like Crazy Lady Vivian." Her voice cracks and she lets out a sob before continuing. "I don't care what any of you say, my father is coming back and he is going to pass right by here."

"I know, I believe ya,"Declan gently rubs her back and shushes her. She seems to regain herself. She softens once again. There is a long awkward silence, and I am beginning to realize there is a lot more to this little girl. Judging from the vibe in the air, this is not the time for me to pry.

"I am completely confused, who the heck is Crazy Lady Vivian," I ask. Declan turns to me with a grateful smile. I feel the tension begin to lift as he appreciates the distraction. Anna relaxes even more, an edge lifts, and her shoulders loosen. I see her starting to slip back to her easy spirit.

"Lady Vivian, where do I start?" Declan reclines gently, as he begins to tell the tale. I lean against the soft grass and look out to the majestic view of the ocean. I can see for miles with glimpses of inlets and long sandy coastlines.

Anna sits straight up allowing her sadness to drift away, now almost gone. I can tell she enjoys this tale, and my excitement builds as I listen to the lilt of his thick Irish accent.

"Once a long while ago, these ruins were a magnificent castle. It stood high on this mountain with a huge population of noble man, as well as loads of serfs and their families. Indentured slaves, perhaps maybe even sentenced to tend to the land.

Maybe Lady Vivian was the maiden of the castle, or maybe she was a serf. No one is sure, but long after everyone else abandoned or was killed, she remained with her two daughters. They had no way of keeping up the massive land and perhaps it was starvation that drove them to madness, maybe the blood on their hands. But crazy, they were, that the locals are certain about. Anyways, Lady Vivian and her daughters would watch, maybe right here on this very spot even. They would wait, always checking out across the horizon, ever patient and ever waiting. For they knew it was just a matter of time. They had lots of time to wait for the trade ships to pass.

Ireland, and this area around here in particular, would have been one of the last bits of land for the ships. People traveled from all over Europe, as well as the Far East. Boats and cargo ships would want to come to rest here. Once they left our waters, they would be on their own, out there..." He hesitates as he points towards the horizon. "Out there, there is nothing but endless sea. Some even thought you would fall off the end of the earth, if you traveled too far.

Pirates frequented these waters. Some pretty unsavory types floated around down there. There would be quite a bit of plundering to be had, for those brave or brutal enough. Some of those ships would surely be worth a king's ransom.

On dark and foggy nights Vivian and her daughters would fill the windows of the castle with lanterns. The crews aboard the massive trade ships would see her lanterns and think it was a safe port."

He points to the huge boulders and rocks that line the cliffs, farther out to sea, dark rocky formations stick out like tiny islands in and around the cliffs.

"Sometimes the strong gale winds, would blow them, other times the legend has it that she would beckon them in with her lanterns. Either way the huge wood vessels would smash against the rocks, splintering and shattering on contact. The impact alone would have killed most, but if that didn't do them in, then there would be only one choice."

He pauses for a moment as he stretches into a more comfortable position. He begins to tell the tale again. "If the crew of the ships weren't ripped to tatters by the sharp rocks, then they had but only one option. They would need to swim."

I looked down to see the huge waves thundering and pounding on the cliff walls, sheer rock that ran straight up and down. There is no way anyone could climb that. The force of the waves alone would crush you. Some of the rocks were so sharp if a swimmer were knocked against those, well they would be impaled, or gutted for sure.

"The water fills down there, and it is particularly deep. If they managed to swim that far, or tread water or stay away from the jagged rocks. All impossible feats no doubt, but let's just say they did get that far. Well, where would they go? Look down, there is no way up from the rocks. Only one possible way out." Declan stops abruptly, he looks toward Anna and together they utter a single word, "DROWN!"

I am intrigued by his story; I can tell many have told this tale. I imagine it has been interpreted and re-invented by many as well. I am a firm defender of women's rights. Why are people always so quick to blame women?

I turn to look Declan square in the eye, rolling my shoulders back I ask, "How do you know Lady Vivian was responsible, maybe they were just awful sailors? Is there any proof? Why do they blame her?"

Declan takes a moment before he responds, "so the story goes and you are right Audrey. One thing to be sure of, no one alive today knows what happened. Legend has it she would constantly be the one who would first loot the scene. She and her daughters were always spotted near the site. Their dingy filled. Those women profited the most when trading wares. Folks say, every time she would run out of things to trade, there mysteriously enough, would be another ship wrecked." Declan ends his story and turns to me, "Well; there you have it, that is the most popular version of the tale."

I notice the indecision in his voice, "One version," I ask hopefully. "Does that mean you have another," I ask. He looks out and leans back "I don't know about back then, but I do know now, that folks around here, they have a way of judging you, thinking the worse about a person. I have spent many a day up here, tending to me Uncle's cow and I have given it some thought. Maybe, just maybe, she wasn't signaling the boats to their death, maybe she was warning them?" I like where he is going with this and add my own thoughts, "What if she thought they were pirate ships, maybe she was keeping the ships from traveling too far down and discovering the inlet to the village? You said yourself; there were some pretty sketchy people on those boats.

For instance, how did everyone in the castle die? Were they raided, murdered and plundered? If that was the case she may have been on her guard, constantly vigilant, afraid for her safety as well as her daughters.

As far as the stuff from off the ships, the wares and treasure, maybe they stumbled across it. Look at how powerful those waves are. If a wooden ship were to crash, it would make sense that stuff would be thrown everywhere.

Of course she was always there. She is probably the only one who lived this far away from the village. It would make sense she would see, or even hear the wrecks. She would naturally pick up stuff. I mean who is going to leave treasure lying around; of course you would pick it up."

We sit in silence for a long time-quietly munching our berries. With the berries all but gone, and my stomach cramping from the sour fruit, I ask one last question, "Whatever happened to Lady Vivian and her daughters?"

Anna speaks up, "You know I don't think anyone ever found out what happened to them." This sends my imagination soaring, daydreaming all kinds of scenarios. One thing is for certain, I am convinced Lady Vivian, must have been a cool woman, I hope it worked out for her.

Standing and stretching my knotted legs, I am the first to speak, "Listen Anna it's getting late, and we have been here a long time. What do you say we head back?" I give her a hand to pull her up, and we say our goodbyes. This time on the way out of the woods, I stay glued to her side.

Deidre greets us at the door. I look at her as if for the first time. Why had I not noticed before how pale and worn out she seems? Her sadness is so obvious; she wears her grief like the sweater Nana knits me every Christmas - tight and binding.

Later, after an enormous dinner, and some time spent with my parents, I retreat to the warm room at the top of the stairs. Lying in the comfortable bed my legs become heavy, tired from our climb. My head swims. The gale force winds begin to howl, rain pounds the roof above me. I am thinking about Lady Vivian, Deidre Byrne and her missing husband, Anna's father and most importantly, Anna. This small stretch of land, surrounded by sea, a place that is thousands of years old. It has so much history, such different and extraordinary lives each lived here through out the centuries. Each life dealt a fate. Not always fairly. I guess not all tales end happily ever after.

Dad catches me in a hug before I hit the landing on the last set of steps. He seems happy to be working again, even if it's just an assignment. He stands taller, his shoulders back. This is an opportunity for him to put back on some of the weight he lost with all the stress from losing his job.

"Hey, Good Morning, if you need to use the computer, better snap to it, I have to head into the office." I can tell he likes the feeling of having a place to go. Not wanting to deal with the hurt and rejection that came last time I checked my messages, or lack of. I am quick to reply, "Thanks Dad, I can check my messages later." Before he leaves, I give a final squeeze and say, "I love you." He looks genuinely surprised. "What, can't a girl tell her father she loves him," I say smiling. The corner of his mouth turns up into a smile. "Yes, a girl can tell her father she loves him, the more the better, and by the way I love you too kid. Your mother is in the kitchen, it is nice if a girl tells her mother she loves her too." I give him a last grab as I head into the kitchen.

My mother is dusting the piano in the sunroom. Grabbing a piece of bacon off the kitchen table, I walk in, "Good Morning sweetheart, did you catch Dad? He was just looking for you." "Yeah, I saw him. Hey Mom what is the scoop on the Byrnes, what happened?" She stops and puts down the old feather duster, she half turns and glances out the window before starting, "Oh, its very sad, I was waiting to get all the details before I told you. Deidre is awfully vague; the poor thing is having an awful time of it. She is still in shock. I know that Carl Byrne was in some kind of accident. He was or is some sort of fisherman, and the rig he was on hit a terrible storm out to sea. They found parts of the boat, and a few of the crew have since washed up on shore. Its tragic really, but there is no evidence of what happened, it's a complete mystery. I can't imagine," she stops talking and I glance out the glass doors, watching the small figure of Anna as she begins the trek across the huge pasture.

"The not knowing, the wondering if the next body that washes up could be your husbands. I can't even imagine. It is heartbreaking. Deidre has been working with your father, and he says she is trying to be strong. This house is... "

Our conversation stops, her voice quiets to a whisper as we watch Anna climb the fence and stamp her feet at the back door. Her small arm waves at us. She pounds the last bit of mud off. My mother is quick to add in a soft voice, "Deidre did say that Anna has been a rock through it all, just incredibly brave." I don't have a chance to answer.

As my mother greets Anna, I think about our conversation at Lady Vivian's castle. I know the truth about exactly how brave Anna is being about her father's death. Bravery has nothing to do with it. She is in complete denial about his accident. From the sound of it so is Deidre, "being a rock" my butt. Anna is expecting her father to come sailing or walking on water at any moment. It is a far more complicated situation then Mom realizes. Looking at them both I am not sure if it is my place to explain what is going on in Anna's head. I think for now anyway I will do something new. I will keep my mouth shut, until I have more information.

Today is the first day that I start my official duties, which consist of, bodyguard, babysitter and general protector of Anna. After a big breakfast, I collect the list of groceries; stuff some colorful euro bills in my bag, along with the leftover coins. I hesitate for a moment, then run over and hug my mom, "I love you Mom." Leaving I see her standing in the hallway, a look of complete shock over her face from my sudden outburst of affection. I wave back through the glass and she mouths, "I love you too." I smile as our footsteps crunch across the stone driveway.

We stop at our spot on the bridge; I search the cove, checking every wave and ripple, looking for anything that resembles what I saw before. "What are you looking for Audrey?" I wait before I answer. A little annoyed, "I don't know, last time I was sitting here I thought I saw something." "Aye, these seas are filled with many creatures, perhaps you'd be spotting a Mermaid, little lassie." She says the last part in an even thicker accent then her usual brogue. "Very funny," I answer sharply, while keeping a keen eye on my reflection in the murky waters below.

First stop, the library, three times a week I will be dropping Anna off. She will be attending some sort of crafty reading time. The library is across the street from the marina, with the children's section facing front. We are among the first few to arrive. Anna gives me a quick wave goodbye and then runs over to some of her friends, who are hastily scooping the best crayons and markers out of the bin.

The room is bright and cheery with stuffed animals and cushy pillows surrounding shelves, each lined with varying size picture books. The floor length windows reflect the ocean and send shadows that dance and flicker across the playful rug. On a sunny day, you would not even need lights on because the sea casts such a bright reflection.

I step out of the library and on to the old cobblestones. Wandering down the windy road that flanks the cove, I pass a number of cafes and pubs. They have round wrought iron tables, and chairs with umbrellas set out for dining. Beyond that a small grocery store. I stop in to pick up a few vegetables and a loaf of bread. I buy a cloth bag because they don't give away plastic bags in Ireland. Rather than pay for each plastic one, I settle on a pretty pale blue one with small flowers. Since this is the first time my parents have trusted me to actually do any food shopping without them in the store, I am careful with my choices. Those huge oversized coins my Mom gave me the other day, turn out to be one euro each, a little more than one U.S. dollar. The smallest bill here is the five. It seems lame to me, carrying around all these heavy over-stuffed coins. I guess my Mom isn't so cheap after all. Either that or she hasn't figured out the coin exchange. This could really work in my favor. Maybe watching Anna this summer will be a sweeter deal than first anticipated.

I head back up the road towards the library. Although the village is small, it is important to keep a general bearing till I learn my way around. Peeking in the library I catch a glimpse of Anna sitting cross-legged on the floor, completely engrossed in the story.

I am about to cross the cobblestone road when I hear the blast of a horn. I forgot to look right, or was I suppose to look left for traffic and I looked right, who the heck knows anymore. I stepped out in front of a car, big deal. Luckily the road is so narrow and crooked; cars are forced to go slow. Apart from some mild humiliation I am uninjured. With virtually no crime in this little village, kids run around unattended all the time, making drivers more aware. In fact, the police don't even wear guns. It may be less dangerous from criminal activity, but I am a little shocked that there is so little parental supervision with all the water and cliffs, and obvious dangers in the natural surroundings. I guess kids have been running around here for thousands of years, so why stop now? I am more sheltered I guess. In North Carolina I am barely allowed to walk half a block to my friends house. I am enjoying having more freedom, so I will keep my mouth shut with a more watchful eye on traffic. The other side of the road abruptly drops off into the basin marina, the only warning being a small cobblestone and brick footpath with a thick, black painted chain dangling between cement posts, randomly placed. A poor attempt to safely divide the sea from the old stone road.

I stand at the very edge of the road looking down to the water drop below. Someone whistling an annoying tune breaks my concentration. I look up to see Declan carrying a toolbox down the ramp to the temporary metal docks. "Hey, Declan, what's up?" He waves. "Hello Audrey, just helping out until my father gets back this afternoon." I am surprised to see him in this setting. "I thought you were a cow handler?" He gives a nervous laugh before answering, "I guess I am a bit of both, you might say." Our awkward silence is cut short. "Come along Declan, I haven't got all day, I'll be needing those tools. "A gruff voice, leads to a man who's back end is half sticking out of a fishing boat cabin, his dirty, stretched out jeans flash a large butt crack. " Eww that is going to stay with me all day," I remark to Declan curling my lip. He laughs and nods as he hurries toward the fishing boat.

The small fish shop is one room. As soon as I enter and take a breath, there is no mistaking what is being sold. The pungent odor knocks me back. The room is small and across the front is a glass display case showing various fish carcasses. A woman pokes her head up from behind the counter, "What can I get you luv?" She is wearing a black rubber apron, thick black gloves, and heavy black rubber boots. Behind her, a man dressed in the same out-fit decapitates and slices fish. It is alarming how fast and good he is at his job. Every once in a while some gruel or fleshy goo shoots off the cutting board and lands on his rubber apron, each leaving a different colored stain. The fish in the case have all different names, John Dory, Plaice, Prawns. The only fish I ever ate were fish like sticks. I am use to seeing them frozen in a bag, closed in a box with a bearded guy in a raincoat on the front.

I try to turn to my list, hoping I can match something with all these funky choices. Staring blankly at the paper for an eternity, I hand it over the counter asking, "do you have any of these?" She smiles a welcoming smile before asking, "Would you be the Americans, that are staying at the Byrnes house?" "Yes," I reply, so happy that we have something in common.

"Well, well, welcome, I am Carol, Deidre's sister in law. This is my husband Joe." He waves his bloody cleaver. I am finding it hard to answer with the noxious fish fumes and the bloody mess splattered around. She busies herself, removing fish from behind the glass and tearing brown paper from the huge roll. "There you are luv, I threw in some heads and tails for your Ma. She can make a nice fish stock. Lovely to meet you, I hope you and your family will be joining us down at the pub on Sunday night for trivia." I smile awkwardly, "Okay thanks, yeah, see ya." I wave and smile all the while backing out of the shop. I am anxious to leave any place of business that looks like something off a crime scene show. I shudder as I think of them knee deep in that bloody carnage every day, that blood thirsty couple is Anna's Aunt and Uncle. Holidays must be a blast with those two.

The smell of fresh baked goods leads me round the corner to the outside street vendors, selling fresh baked goods. Chocolate squirts into my mouth, as I bite into a fresh croissant, licking each bit of powdered sugar off my fingers while trying to balance my cloth sack, now filled with the very distinct stench of fresh fish. I sit on the quay wall and dangle my feet over the edge, a perfect vantage point to the library windows and the activities inside. Anna is still engrossed in her library pursuits. Some of the kids are prancing; some are on all fours, while others are on tiptoes with their arms in the air fingers curled. Whatever they are up to is fine with me because it gives me a chance to enjoy this amazing croissant.

Taking a slow walk along the sidewalk, it is hard not to be awe struck with the new sites and sounds in and around this foreign land. The sea alone in the basin is the most beautiful shade of teal.

"There it is again," I screech. An older woman riding a bicycle with a basket, wearing a long stretched out cardigan gives me a sideway glance as she turns her bike wheel slightly away and continues past. This time the creature is just below the waters surface. It skims past fast. I make out its torpedo shape. It rolls onto its back; and pokes it shiny sleek head out of the water. Looking me directly in the eye is an adorable seal. Before I make an audible sound I look around to make sure no one is around. " Ooh, you are so cute. What are you doing here," I ask. It flips around again and dives into the water. "Don't go." I plead but it's too late. I am talking to a ribbon of small waves.

Quickly, I grab a chunk off my croissant and throw it down, where it last surfaced but nothing. I wait and try again, this time throwing a smaller piece; the water remains calm and quiet. I throw the cloth sack onto the pavement. Riffling through I find the fish, tearing at the tape and ripping through the brown paper I finally find what I need. It's eye stares back at me. Yuck, I grab it with my index finger nail and pinky nail. I aim and drop it between the two pieces of croissant, floating waterlogged. It bobs and floats on the tiny wake for a while, the milky eye still stares back menacingly. After a moment, the water around the head shimmers a silvery, gray, in an instance a little mouth pokes up, and the head is gone.

"Unbelievable, I saw that," I say as I clap my hands together and stretch my feet. "A seal, I just gave a fish head to a seal." The seal does one more quick turn, dives out towards the middle of the basin marina, and is gone. "You're welcome," I yell to its retreating figure.

Feeling thrilled as I jump up and gather the groceries that are strewn across the cobblestone path. I wipe a dirt spot off the bread and stuff it in to the bag. Some of the children are already exiting the library. Looking to my left, or did I look to the right for traffic.

Anyway, I am greeted with a blast from a car horn; I have once again forgotten that the traffic comes from the other side. "Yeah, yeah, I see you, American in training," I shout as I cross to the other side.

Anna looks up and sees me waving and talking to the driver of the car, "Friend of yours?" she asks. Walking home I stop at where I had seen the seal. "Right here I was sitting right here." I point to the spot. "When all of a sudden a seal came in, right there, I couldn't believe it. It was definitely what I saw in the sea the other day. I couldn't believe it came up so close." I am so excited as I tell Anna, I can see the happiness spread over to her. "I have never seen one that close." Her enthusiasm is genuine; she is truly thrilled for me. I am not accustomed to a "friend" being really happy for me. Usually they just act it, but it seems like their eyes tell a different story, mostly laced with jealousy and contempt. I grab her in a tight hug and swing her around. She hugs me tightly, " Come on I have to get you back home, and hey by the way I met your Aunt and Uncle." I don't mention I have seen horror movies with less blood then their fish shop. Also, I leave out the part about how I fed the seal a fish head her aunt gave me. I hope it isn't something sacred in Irish culture. You know like in India they worship the cow.

Chapter 5

Anna enjoys the days we head into town. She is light and fresh and we often linger in the harbor looking for the seal. Sharing my fish parts trick with her, I demonstrate how I lure the seal out of hiding. Anna is a great help at getting all kinds of fish entrails from her Aunt and Uncle. I am glad to see there is no harm in giving the parts away, although her Aunt has commented that my mother makes an incredible amount of fish stock. Which always leaves Anna falling onto the display case in a fit of giggles. Her Uncle looks up from his bloody fish carnage to smile, "its nice to hear that again, my lady, it's been awhile." He looks back to his spoils cutting and pruning, peeling back skin to form neat fillets.

Anna breaks into another fit of laughter, when I throw a fish head out into the basin, she stares intently as the creature darts in and out and floats on his back. He puts on a little show, before he devours his lunch. Some days the seal will hangout with us, social and silly. Other days without any warning he will surface grab the head and then be gone.

The seal is beginning to trust me. Most days, he will emerge as soon as I sit and put my legs over the edge. Usually playful and a showoff, he swirls and churns the water forming his own little wake which allows the bait to bob and weave. Then he jumps and pulls most of his body out of the water while grabbing the food. Always succeeding in hitting us with a small splash of ocean, just a bit with his tail.

Other days the seal seems much more reserved cautiously waiting to be fed. On these days he is much less playful and only shows his gratitude with a quick dive, or a small splash. Anna enjoys our time together on the dock, regardless of whether we see a seal.

Tonight I am exhausted. Sleep creeps up on me during dinner. I decide to head up early with my book. The fresh sea air, the continued treks into town and the castle have worn me out.

I climb under the covers, warm and soft. My body instantly relaxes. It isn't long before I feel myself drop into a sleep like state. My mind falls farther still into suspended restless dreams. Each one more realistic than the last: fragments of stories, beckoning to me from far away and long ago.

The stone is cold on my bare feet. Opening a heavy wooden door with a huge iron knob immediately floods me in beautiful warm sunlight. The garden is full with rows of green. A goat peers its head over the wall made of stone that is white washed and pristine. Running my hand along a huge boulder I slide it over the familiar crevice. Slippery and cool, my fingers ride along it like a miniature slide. The goat makes an attempt to grab at some of our vegetables, growing just inside the wall. I swing my arms at him angrily. The animal is so comfortable with me, it doesn't feel threatened at all, and slowly turns back to the tall grass and thistle, not the least bit impressed with my scolding. I walk through the rows of food growing in abundance. My hand catches on a weed. It stings at the spot between the thumb and forefinger. It is beginning to bubble and burn. I hurry to the corner of the garden, on the other side of the stone enclosure, where the tiny saplings are freshly planted. I pull up a weed with a yellow flower on it. Quickly, I rub the bud over the sting and with in seconds the welt is barely visible and the pain is gone. Leaning against my favorite rock, the perfect diamond shape makes a comfortable seat. I look out over our massive grounds and farther out to the cliffs that drop into the sea.

It is then I hear the voice, it's a whisper mostly. I can't make out the words. I strain to hear, but it is no use, I can't quite understand. The sun is so warm on my face.

I wake with a jolt. The sun is streaming through the paper blinds and heating my cheek. I am back in the slanted ceiling bedroom on the top floor. The dream I just left was unlike any I have ever had before. It was so real and so detailed. Lying in bed for a while I try to piece together every brief moment of it. I hear my mother talking downstairs to Anna. Her voice sounds excited. I am sure she has another day of adventure in store.

"What do you have in mind, today," I ask her. "Guess," she smiles. After a long lazy breakfast, Anna and I begin to prepare for the days outing. I pull on my faithful wellie boots. I never know what the weather holds but I am confident these will suit. She turns at the driveway and begins to head up. Normally a trip to the old castle ruins would be my first pick, but today I am feeling a little tired and lag behind as we start the strenuous hike up to Vivian's castle.

Anna runs to her usual spot, I choose to linger around the old ruins. It is beginning to feel so familiar and comfortable here. I enjoy piecing together the lay out of the old castle. So far this is my favorite spot in Ireland. I walk through the tangle of boulders.

My peaceful morning is rudely interrupted by the sound of shouts. I can just make out the outline of three boys approaching Anna from the other side. Judging from their distant outlines, they look to be about her size and stature. They are moving through the tall grass faster than I can. They have converged on her, as she sits on the small path. Quickening my step, I am nearly in a full run, tripping over the tall grass, I am still able to come up on her other side, undetected.

"Move," the larger boy, in the group of three shouts at her. "Excuse me, can I help you," I ask, glaring down at the little squirt. "Who are you," he demands, looking surprised and a little scared by my presence. Before I have a chance to reply Anna chimes in. "Get out of here Timmy."

"Make me, idiot," he replies, but with his thick accent, it comes out more sounding like "ijiet". He looks up to me and adds. "Who is this another one of your gypsy relatives? Look lads, its one of Anna's tinker cousins." He laughs and turns back to his group of little thugs. "What is with the accent? You tinker trash sure get around."

I am not sure what he means and I am beginning to get angry with the little punk. I begin to move in when out of nowhere a crow, well more like a raven swoops down. It barely misses his head. If I didn't know better I would swear it was aiming right at him. Losing his footing he falls backwards on to the path. "Smooth there, Slick." I add as he brushes himself off quickly.

He looks like he is going to start in again when I take the opportunity to point out the brown stain that is forming on the back of his pants. "You may want to clean that up, it looks like you had a bit of a spill if you know what I mean." I add. This sends a shiver of laughter through the gruesome twosome that is standing behind him. They elbow each other and one says, "Ya Tim, it looks like you crapped your knickers."

This makes the pasty boy's face turn two shades of red. Glaring back at me, he turns on his heel and heads back the way he came. "Come on lads." He shouts to his gang as he sends one last burning look my way. "Who was that," I ask. Anna shakes her head. "Timmy Fielding and just some stupid lads from school." She doesn't seem too upset by the group.

I have dealt with my own share of complete creeps and bullies at school. So I opt to let it go with, "What a bunch of losers."

Crossing over Anna, I start down the path after them. I want to see where the little derelicts are headed. The last thing I want is for them to decide to come back. They are moving pretty fast, completely comfortable with the cliffy terrain. Passing my hands over the tall grass I try to keep pace, but they are flying and it is obvious I will never catch them.

Suddenly I am stung. The burn moves quickly up my hand and white bubbles form, where the pain grows intense. "Ouch." I begin to blow and rub it when Anna runs towards me. "It's a nettle sting, don't rub it." "What kind of bug is a nettle?" I whimper. "It hurts way worse than any bee sting."

"Just nettles, Audrey, stop rubbing it, you are making it worse." "What the heck are these," I ask, "Are they on me I feel something trying to land, do you hear buzzing, I think its in my hair." I feverously try to shake them out convinced they are nesting in my hair. "It's a plant, not a bug," she answers trying to subdue a laugh. "A plant what is it like some kind of fly trap does it clamp down on you? Does it have jaws that borough into your skin?" She tries to keep a straight face, walking over to a pretty nondescript weed. In fact it looks like any ordinary houseplant. She points down at it. "Look, its just something you will have to get familiar with. They are everywhere out here. Some of the older lads even have contests to see who can eat the most before their tongue swells up." I look back at her with a sarcastic questioning face. "You can try spitting on it, some swear it works, others try to rub more nettle over it, but all I have ever seen that do is make it worse. My best advice is to just forget about it, as soon as you stop thinking about it, it won't hurt so bad, no bother." With that she turns and heads to her spot where she sits. "No bother, no bother," I shake my head as I mimic her accent, "For you, Anna, maybe its no bother, but I will tell you what, for me it's a bother, it's a big bother. It freaking hurts." My complaints are falling on deaf ear. She is trekking back towards her secret spot.

Looking at my hand, it is between my thumb and forefinger. It hits me, this is just like the dream I had last night. I run back towards the castle. Everything, everywhere I look its just like I saw last night. In the dream this was a garden, with the walls made of stone. Only its not like the dream, everything was new and clean, and in tact last night. Now everything is old and gone. The stones aren't white anymore and there are only a few left in a line, the rest lay in piles. But I can see it.

I look to where the small sapling was, now a massive tree. I run beneath it. I know exactly what I need. I search the ground, walking bent over while searching, its not here. It was just a dream, what am I doing? I give up hope because my hand is throbbing now. Heading back to the path, I see the tiny blossom. Near where the wall was, the one that use to stand right here, it once had a great wooden door that lead to it. I know because I walked through it last night in my dream. Bending down I grab the small blossom and rub it on my sting. The pain is gone. I knew it would be, my dream told me so. I rest back on the diamond shaped rock, trying to make sense of everything. I must be going nuts. It must be a coincidence. I need to get a grip and sort out, the logical explanation to this. My hand slides across the smooth surface of the rock it knows exactly where to rest, finding the crevice on the boulder my fingers glide over the tiny slide. Just like it has done before.

Chapter 6

Sitting at the dinner table, I debate whether to tell my parents. How do I even start? "Oh by the way, I may or may not be having some sort of paranormal time travel." I daydream about the media finding out, "Kelly, Jack, your daughter may be a time traveler, or psychic." I can just see the paparazzi swarming outside my door, to get a picture of the "freak of nature" kid. My face plastered all over everyone's homepage, the news and on the magazines at the check out of the supermarket. I can just imagine the kids at school, "Can you see the answers on the math test?" These thoughts occupy me, all through dinner, and as we sit down to television later. I can tell my Mom is curious about what is distracting me. This is when I wish the adoption would have happened. I need a little sister or brother to take some of the heat off me. Every time I look up she is staring at me. Finally she asks, "Are you okay, honey?" I try to smile, and after an agonizing hour, I say, "Wow, ten o'clock already, I am going to bed, goodnight." With that, I excuse myself and am out of there.

It is impossible to will myself back to the dream I had last night. After two hours trying I give up. I push the gray bar on top of the primitive clock. The bedside table lights with a neon green haze.

12:08 am: I start with mild paranoia. Maybe I was possessed. Maybe there is a ghost right here in the house. This leads to a random search of the closet and under the bed. "How lame was that," I ask myself out loud. If there were something in the house, why would it be in a dream?

Which leads me to re-analyze the dream. It was pretty vague. I have always had an interest in medieval times. Is it possible my subconscious created the whole thing? The outline of the castle was there in the ruins. Rooms were still partially laid out in stone. I could have mentally put together the blueprint, re-built it and cleaned it up. That's sort of how dreams work, reality mixed with fantasy. I rub my hand. The bumps are barely even there, just a light impression. Could it be just a coincidence? I have an explanation for the whole thing and I close my eyes again, this is silly. Imagination, it does have a way of getting out of control.

I hit the button. The clock reads 12:22am. How do I explain the yellow flower? How did I know to go for it? I go back and forth in my head to answer this question. Did, I hear it, or read it somewhere? I could have then stored the information in the recesses of my mind. The brain is a fascinating machine, I have heard about repressed memories. The practical side of me kicks in once again. There is a logical answer for everything. I have never really believed in ghosts or omens. Scary movies are pretty lame. I am not one to entertain the possibility of anything supernatural.

1:16 am. How did I know to look in the small stone garden for the flower? It wasn't where the dream had told me it would be. It was fairly close though....

3:48 am. What about the stone? I mean how did I know right where the hidden crevice was, and the way it formed that little slide...

The morning light has been streaming into my room for a few hours. I no longer have to use the tiny night-light to see the time. I am exhausted. I spent the entire night, imagining what the dream could have meant. Reading into every aspect of it, and then rationalizing the facts. My only conclusion, I need to get more information. I may have experienced something supernatural, or I may have an incredibly active imagination.

My mother takes one look at me and gasps. "Sweetheart are you okay?" She runs over and puts her hand on my forehead. "You don't have a fever. Do you feel nauseas?" "Mom, I am fine, I just didn't sleep well. I will nap later. I promise." With that I head into the kitchen. She follows closely behind, practically on top of me. Parents, or moms in particular, get a notion you aren't feeling well and they ride you like last years cheap swimsuit.

"Oh, listen Audrey, I am using the computer today to do some work, do you want to check e-mails before I get started?" I have more important things on my mind today, so I am quick to reply. " No thanks Mom. Can I check them later?" She looks genuinely surprised, and now she is convinced I have contracted some sort of fatal virus, she moves in even closer, if that is possible."

I try to divert her attention. " Hey, Mom do you know what a tinker is? Some kid called Anna's family one yesterday. I got the impression the boys were trying to make her mad?" I told her I thought it had do with some kind of Irish gypsy. We decide to check it out online. She fires up the computer and we wait for the system to boot up.

My mother and I often check out something together on the computer, either a cool topic, or strange word. Its kind of geeky I know but its not like I would share it with any one from school.

She immediately pulls up a page and begins reading aloud. "Travellers the preferred modern term. In the past the terms used were tinkers or gypsies. Often referred to as The Other of the Irish." She pulls on her glasses and reads quietly for a minute before adding; " it says here they are a transient minority group who choose to move around as oppose to staying in one area. They have been part of the Irish culture for the last 800 years or so. The group prefers to be self-employed. They often set up camps along roads or in fields, although occasionally they do own houses." She looks up from the computer. "Wow Audrey, there is so much history and culture here that I wasn't even aware of." My mother stops talking abruptly as Anna's face appears at the back glass. I signal Anna to come in with a wave, as my mother slowly closes out the page, and puts the computer to sleep. "We can check it out later Mom, thanks." I kiss the top of her head, as I motion for Anna to join us.

"Do you girls want me to drive you into town today? I have the car." I nod, "sure that would be great Mom." I know how my mom's mind works. If I let her drive us into to town she will have more time to monitor my health. It will prevent her from worrying. I eat a magnificent breakfast and top it off with a huge serving of fruit. I can see her body relaxing and she stops staring at me. When my mother thinks I am even slightly run down she moves into stalker mode.

I tuck my tee shirt into my jeans and comb my tasseled hair in the front mirror while my mother grabs the ringing phone. I tie on my black converse sneakers with the bright pink laces. Anna pulls on her boots and we head out to the car. My mother walks to my side of the car, thinking it's the driver's side door. She over exaggerates her shoulder shrug and heads to the other side, which has the steering wheel. We laugh at how confusing the driving is to us. "Girls, that was Anna's mom who called. She is working late tonight, so when you finish up in town could you take Anna home? Oh and Audrey can you pick up some tea for her Grandmother at the store?" "Sure, Mom listen I know you have to pick up Dad from work tonight. I can grab something to eat with Anna if you two want to go out?"

My mother looks over surprised. "Thanks Audrey. That sounds great."

Anna shows my mother a short cut to get to the library. It brings us up onto the backside of the village. A small spring widens into a rocky shallow channel of marshy water. I can make out the stone bridge we cross about a mile down. I notice two horses crudely tied and grazing close to the road. They look like painted pintos mixed with a working breed, like a draft horse. They are stocky and bulky. Their chunky legs taper down to the fetlocks with the feathering fur covering the hoof. The white part of their body is mostly turned gray with sooty patches, from lack of grooming.   They are grazing the tall grass that grows between the road and sidewalk. It is so strange to see horses so close to the road, unsupervised and unfenced. I see a number of old trailers parked back to back ahead. There are small bicycles and toys strewn around. A makeshift laundry line hangs from a trailer the other side tied down on to a tree. Pants and shirts in various sizes hang. A skinny dog lumbers around slowly, sniffing the ground.

I glance over at my mother and she looks back and nods. Sharing an unspoken thought. We know we are looking at a traveller's camp. So similar to what we have just seen on the computer. I glance back at Anna who smiles at me. I can see the bridge that I walked over countless times. It stands right in front of us. You can't miss what lies on the other side of the bridge; it has been here the whole time. I had never even noticed this whole other world. I have been so busy looking for the seal, or looking at the marina, or worse yet my own reflection. Even if I had seen it, I am not sure it would have registered. This is someone's home. I have to crane my neck to see it as we pull up towards the roundabout that leads to the library.

In front of the library we slow to a stop. Anna jumps out taking a quick second to thank my mom. She trots into the glass doors and over to the children's section with a group of other kids. My mother grabs my arm to slow me from jumping out. "Don't judge them Audrey, I know its hard not to make assumptions but we don't know them. We are just visiting." It is obvious she is talking about the traveller's. She knows me so well. "I won't Mom. I'll see you later, and thanks." We both know I am grateful for more than just the ride. I am thanking her for always making sure I keep my mind open. She has made a point to tell me, my whole life, that people are allowed to be different. She is a firm believer in live and let live.

Racing in behind Anna, I mouth I will see you later before heading over to the non-fiction section. I have always been comfortable in a library. I love books and I enjoy research. Again, another bit of information I wouldn't share with a lot of people. This village library is not much bigger than my middle school media center.

Where do I start, hmmm...the travellers are fascinating and I am interested in their story, no doubt, but what I really want to know about is the castle's back-story, and more importantly Lady Vivian.

I sit down at the computer, and rub my hands together. Okay, where do I start? I type a jumble of letters a number of times before erasing what I have written and starting again.

Castles of Ireland pops up on the screen. That should be a good place to start. Up comes a list of about one hundred castles. Unbelievable, this place was loaded with them. I check the county; I check the village, nothing even remotely close. Then I try Vivian, nothing, and then ladies in waiting, still blank. I find a section on local history and decide I should do my search the old - fashioned way. I head over to the shelf and pull four or five books. I stumble a bit under the weight of my find, finally making it to the sets of tables. There is a woman behind the circulation desk who has taken a particular interest in me. I glance over and smile before digging head long in.

The information around the time Vivian and the castle were here are vague at best. The fourth century someone built a friary where the village now is, then in the seventh century a church came, and King James of England built a castle to fortify the village. Still I find no mention of the castle up on the bluff. It doesn't seem likely the King of England would build a castle down here if he knew one was up on the cliff looking down at him. So chances are it wasn't here yet, or it was already down. Here is something cool, the small bridge that takes Anna and I over the water and into the village was built by the Dukes of Devonshire. Maybe she was with them. I am at a stand still. I sit back and put my hands behind my head. I close my eyes, opening them again to the sound of gentle breathing at my desk. "May, I help you with something, luv?"

I open my eyes to see the keeper of the circulation desk, a woman in a flowered dress and heavy stockings, leaning over my makeshift pile of books. Curiosity must have gotten the best of her. Because after watching me from her perch at the front of the library, she has finally relented. I wonder what the final straw was. What was it that gave her that last bit of courage that enabled her to wander over?

"Yes, I think that you can help me." I answer pausing a little as I figure out the best way to ask this. "The castle, you know the one on the top of the cliff?" I point out the window. "The ruin up there, I am interested in finding out about it." She smiles. "Oh, you mean Lady Vivian's?" "Yes, that's the one. Would you have information on it, anything at all?" She stares at me a second, "Are you American?" I am not really sure what that has to do with my question but I nod, "Yes, I am, my father is here working for the summer, and we are renting a house from the Byrnes." I look towards the children's section, "Anna Byrne." I have learned enough in the last few weeks, that it is best to introduce yourself right away. I don't want to be confused with one of the tourists that I have seen hanging around town. She may not give me all the information if she thinks I am going to just be here for a short time. Visitors sail in here for a weekend and then head out again as quickly as they came. If she thinks I am a tourist she will close up like a clam. I won't get the time of a day out of her. I have seen that for myself. I have also noticed Anna's family name carries a lot of clout around here. I am not sure if it is because of the stuff with her Dad or because she seems to be related to everyone. Whatever it is, it works and I am beginning to use it.

"Oh right, well welcome to the area dear, are you enjoying your visit?" "Yes, I am thank you for asking." We both pause, looking at each other for a second. "Very good, now Lady Vivian and the castle, that's what you are interested in? Folks say she was crazy, did you know that? Well I am afraid I can't help you with that my dear, the fire and all, sad story. Sad story, indeed."

She looks out the window and shakes her head. "Fire? Was there a fire up at the castle," I ask. I am becoming totally confused. "I don't remember hearing about a fire?" She cuts me off. "Oh, no luv, the fire was here, in town." Again, she stops and just shakes her head. I am thoroughly lost now.

"There was a fire in town? I am sorry to hear about that, I hope everyone was okay? But what I am wondering about is finding out any information on the castle." I can tell it is going to take some work to keep this woman on track. "I am sorry luv, I guess I am not making myself very clear, dear. The fire was in the rectory. The whole place burned, it smoked and charred for days. They think it might have been arson, they never did find out who started it. Some say it was a couple of lads who had broken into the church and were trying to cover up their crime. Covering their tracks perhaps. Those were desperate times. Some say it was poor folks, freezing and starved. Probably half crazed, it was during the potato famine. We lost most of the population in the village. We did indeed. Those were desperate times. Well, the records were all kept in the church and they all went up. Nothing left. It was a terrible time, people starving in the streets." Again she shakes her head and looks out the glass windows onto the calm sea. "Well dear, I am afraid all the written records went in the fire, nothing left." I can tell by the expression on her face something had made it through the fire and famine. It was smeared all over her. It was the suffering and sadness that the famine brought. I read it on her face as clearly as I read the words in the books that lay before me in her library.

"Thank you very much." I manage to say, in a defeated whisper. I gently fall back in the chair. I had not given it a second thought, until now. I look and read. The potato famine, I had just leafed through the history books, turning the pages over it. Too busy trying to find Lady Vivian. Casually skimming the pages not paying any attention to the lives that must have been affected. These were probably Anna's own relatives. Regardless of whose relatives they were. They were people and they suffered horribly.

I glance at the huge clock on the wall-I barely have time to run to the store to get the tea. I relay the books back to their shelves and head out the door. The cove is seeing a steady increase in boat traffic and I realize I won't have time to visit the seal today. "Sorry buddy," I whisper as I dash over to the grocery store to grab the tea before sprinting full speed. I scarcely make it back in time to pick up Anna.

The walk home was particularly quiet. First, I notice the craftsmanship on the bridge. I imagine the Dukes of Devonshire maneuvering the huge boulders and arching them over the waterway below. The manpower and sheer strength that was involved is mind blowing. I glance over at the trailers, taking a moment to think about the life of a traveller. Living on the fringes of town, never feeling accepted –moving on to the next spot. I stand for a moment, turning back to get a full view of the village. I can't even begin to think what starvation must be like. A whole community dying during the potato famine: I try to imagine all the people from my town not having any food. The weak and young people dying first. "Are you okay?" Anna's question snaps me out of my heavy thoughts. "Sorry, yeah. I was just thinking about something I read."

I quickly try to shake off these thoughts. I want to go back to my simple thoughts. It is hard to let go of the truth. The fact that so many people have to overcome so many huge obstacles. It has been easy to read about something in a book - some sad event that took place in some far away place, some long time ago. But to be here is different. To walk the same paths, to actually see it with my own eyes, the trailers, the stonework, the village, it makes me realize. These are not just stories in a book. These are lives.

Chapter 7

I am curious to see where it is that Anna disappears to when she leaves our place everyday. We wind up on the road, past the house we are renting, around the corner, and down a thin little drive that opens to a courtyard of sorts. She pushes two black small gates, which gives access to a cobblestone square. I can imagine how it would have easily held multiple carriages at one time. An entrance to a stable lies to our right. The house is set back, a massive stone structure. It must be a couple hundred years old at least. The way it sits makes it impossible to see from the road. Which is deceptive because it boasts an incredible view of the countryside, below and above it. It is gray stone with white shutters. There is an enormous set of wood double doors but Anna choses to go around to the side. She climbs a couple of steps to enter through a smaller door, into a kitchen.

Wiping my feet from the muddy cobblestone court before following her in to a huge kitchen. The floor is covered in small red tiles. The cupboards are huge with a massive enamel oven taking up most of one wall. It has four little doors along the front side for baking with two large round trays on top that act as burners. There is a delicious smell permeating from the oven that is beginning to fill the room.

Leaving the tea on the table I follow Anna as she takes a door along the back wall. We head into a long corridor with doors on every side. It is a warm day, but there is a chill in the house. A cold dampness accompanied with a musty smell, greet us as we move down the long hall.

"Gram are you here," Anna calls as she continues down farther still. "Back here luv," I hear a voice from the distance. "Anna, this house is massive," I say as I try to keep up. The hallway seems to go on forever. "Its my Grandma's. This is the house my mother grew up in. We have been staying here," an awkward pause lingers in the air, before Anna finishes "lately." We turn right into a large room. Judging from the size of it, it could have been almost a ballroom. Today, it acts as a family room. Multiple couches all in different colors and patterns line the edges. A small coffee table sits in the middle, flanked by a large fireplace with a smaller inset within. It is burning a black coal fire sprinkled with wood. The wood occasionally pops and sparks while the underlying coal gives a dusty feel to the room.

Declan is sitting on the couch next to an ancient woman. Anna goes over and kisses her on the cheek. "This is Audrey, Grandma." The woman beckons me closer. "Hello, dear come in." I walk over and shake her hand. She is a solid looking woman with strong features. Her hair is white, with a blue hue. Her light blue eyes have a milky haze over them. The skin on her hand is paper thin and veiny, but she delivers a firm handshake. She is wearing a white heavy cardigan.

"A pleasure to meet you, your home is lovely." I use the word "lovely" because that is what everyone in town says, I immediately regret it, as I take a few steps back. "Hi, Audrey, how are you?" Declan stands adding, "How about some tea?" "Lovely son that would be perfect. Anna help your cousin, with some tea. Audrey, you come over and keep me company while the kids put the kettle on." I sit down next to her, trying to distance myself from the warm fire. The house may be damp, but it is the middle of summer, and I am beginning to feel over heated already.

"Now dear, all the way from America, you have traveled far." She is quiet for a moment, before adding,

"I never met an American I didn't like, that is true." She smiles to herself.

I smile back at her and stare towards the doorway, willing Declan and Anna back. We sit quietly for a minute. Anna's grandmother seems completely at ease with our silence, and I can feel her eyes checking me over, as if I am some sort of exotic animal at the zoo. "How are you?" I ask attempting to break the staring and silence. "I am...I am old, don't let anyone tell you anything different dear, being old is tough. It sneaks up on you. Catching you when you are not looking. It grabs you with both hands."

I laugh nervously at this remark, I can see where Anna gets her ability to be so real. It is rare for me to hear someone talk so honest.

It is not long until I hear the clinking of china in the hallway. Declan enters carrying a tray with a delicate set of china. A small pot is steaming with tea, and four small cups with saucers accompany, all resting on top of a white linen tea towel. He places the tray on the coffee table. Anna slips in behind carrying a platter of all different kinds of cookies. "Lovely, lovely, biscuits too. Help yourself darling." Grandma says radiantly, genuinely excited over the prospect of cookies.

I sit uncomfortably as I thank her. I think I may have even called her Ma'am. Which brings a further smile to her face. Her bony gnarled fingers pour a shaky cup of tea, which she passes to me. "Please call me Grandma." Anna grabs a cup of tea, a handful of cookies and heads out of the room across the hall. A few moments later, I hear the television go on. Shortly after the theme song to some American cartoon permeates in quietly.

Grandma sits back with her tea, and looks me straight in the eye. "You have been spending a lot of time with Anna. Does she mention her father? Did she tell you he was dead?" I cough a little at the last question, before I look over towards Declan. He smiles slightly out of the corner of his mouth while shaking his head.

Grandma wastes no time before she tells me about Carl, Anna's father. She explains how he was always pushing the envelope. It was rough weather but those boys headed out anyway. Then she tells me Deidre needs to be honest with that child. She seems to think Deidre is allowing Anna to keep the notion he is alive. This old woman doesn't beat around the bush. I guess when you get to be her age, you can call it the way you see it.

I admire her, once again I see that strength I have liked so much in Anna. Declan excuses himself to get more firewood, which leaves us alone. I sit awkwardly for a moment, trying to think of something to say to fill the time before Declan comes back. "Your house is beautiful, it is so large." She nods. "It was a mess. My husband and I were so young back then. You think you can do anything. Michael, my husband's father owned all this land. As far as the eye can see, this house was wasting away right in the middle of it all. Not fit for pigs. It wasn't. It took years to put this house back together. It had belonged to a British Lord. Left in a hurry, at least we think he left. The British weren't exactly on good terms with us back then. He may have been killed here, not really sure about that?" With this she lets out a scary half laugh. "It took us years to rebuild, the place. The kids were all born here."

Her voice is soothing, and the fire warmth covers me like a soft throw. I can barely keep my eyes open, slowly they become too heavy, and close. She tells me about her five children. How proud she is of each of them. One is a banker in Dublin. One is a doctor in England, and Deidre is going back into engineering.

71

Her youngest son is a farmer, he must be the one who has the cows, up at the castle, that Declan looks after. Her youngest daughter Mary sounds like a handful. I wonder where Declan fits in.

"She was always getting into something, that Mary," Grandma says. A distinct fondness is apparent in her voice. "She saved us all you know, that one did." I open my tired burning eyes. "Saved you?" My interest peaked. "We were down to our last few bob. With five hungry kids, it was tough times. Well, wouldn't you know that Mary she found a treasure. That girl comes home one day and brings us a pile of gold and gems. The old lord must have stashed all his finery. Whoever that belonged to we never figured out. Whoever it was, hid it up in the hills near the old castle. Tucked away in an underground cellar. It is so overgrown up there. It was just waiting for our precious Mary to find it. I still don't know how she ever did it. Saved us all that one did. A real shame though, she went and married that scoundrel, that's where her trouble started that awful man. That's the reason she ran off. It was him that drove her away."

Grandma stories are hard to follow. Like the librarian she skips around a lot. I can't tell if this is because of their age, or just me not understanding the accent. Either way, I am having trouble following.

I wonder if this has something to do with the kids who were teasing Anna. Declan enters with twigs to add to the coal fire. "Declan looks just like his Mum. Mary is a beauty, no doubt about that." Judging from the confusion on his face, I would say he didn't hear much of the conversation. "I know Grandma." Declan smiles with a distant pain. I sit back on the couch and look out the huge windows to the countryside below. Looking away, keeps me from seeing the hurt in his eyes.

Draining the last of the tea from my cup, I think about all the stories. Some many sad stories, so much pain. Does anyone around here have just an ordinary life? I am blown away by everything I have heard and seen and read. I can only imagine where Mary, Declan's mother has gone off to. The warm tea mixed with the fire, the comfortable couch, and the lack of sleep, take their toll. My eyes close, it is impossible to keep them open. I struggle to hold on but sleep finally wins.

The room is dark and freezing. I reach for my wrap. I hear the shuffling of layers of cloth, the swishing of a skirt. Light appears in the doorway. I slowly move towards the fire's light. A voice is speaking in hush tones. My heart is racing. I strain to hear what she is saying. I can't make out the words. Her back is to me. She is carrying a torch moving gracefully through the keep and into the Great Hall. I am quick to follow. She moves effortlessly into the dark cavernous hallways. "Where are we going," I ask barely able to keep up with her. "Hurry." Her voice is a shrill. She is in a panic. She moves too quickly, her long raven hair is illuminated by the torch, I can see her clearly now. I reach for her touching her skirt. "They need our help. The ships have returned, and they are taking more."

I wake with a jolt. Anna is leaning over me. I am back in Grandma's house, back in the warm family room. "Who needs help?" Anna asks. "I don't know. I am not sure?" I hear my voice answering Anna. I still feel such a panic, a genuine fear. The dream just like the last time. Is so real. I could feel the cloth on her dress. I can't seem to shake it off. It takes a moment for my eyes to focus and my heartbeat to slow down. I am in Anna's grandmother's manor house. I am safe. Anna is looking at me with the weirdest stare. I piece together what happened before the dream. I was by the fire. I was talking to Grandma. I fell asleep. I look over but the seat where Anna's grandma was sitting is vacant. I rub my eyes as I look out the massive windows, to see the shadows growing longer. I speak to Anna, but I am talking to myself, "Just some dream, I guess?"

Anna smiles, "Are you hungry? Dinner is ready, and Grandma is not going to let you out till you have your fill." I follow Anna into the kitchen. The table is piled with trays of food. It is obvious Grandma still cooks for a large family, even if they have long since gone.

Deidre is busy setting the table. She gives me a warm welcome mixed with the beautiful smell from the oven. I begin to feel safe again. I had not realized how hungry I was. It feels good to put the dream away, out of my mind, at least for a little while.

The food starts being passed, one delicious platter after another. A beautiful roast, some glazed carrots and parsnips, and the potatoes. There are mountains of them. Some are roasted, some baked, it's a feast. I am blown away at how good everything tastes. I notice immediately that three generations are sitting together and truly enjoying each other's company. They have a keen interest in each other's day and are quick to bring me into their warm conversation. I help with the clean up, which is also a family affair; everyone pitches in to clear the feast.

"Come along Audrey, I will walk you back. I need to walk some of that dinner off." Deidre says. I am glad for the company, I am nervous to walk back alone. "I am sure my mum was filling your head with all kinds of stories. She is quite a character, that woman." Deidre says proudly.

I walk quickly behind her. It is not the stories Grandma told me that has me so jittery tonight. It was the dream, not even just the dream. It was the fear, the panic that I felt. I pull my hood up trying to keep the fear from finding me again.

"I am blown away by all the history, and stories," I say. Trying to be cautious with my words, "I knew it was old here, but I didn't expect so much... I don't know drama." Saying that I look up at the massive house, now just a dark shadow. Deidre stops for a moment and looks back to me, "Drama, that's a good way of putting it, we have definitely had our share of drama." Suddenly embarrassed, I hope she doesn't think I mean about her husband. I make a pathetic approach at an apology. I explain that I was talking about the house, and the treasure Mary found. Then I realize she probably thinks I mean about Mary running off. I am flustered and tongue tied again.

She turns around quickly. "Audrey, don't worry about it. My sister Mary has quite a reputation in these parts. She is a lovely woman. She uncovered a mass of antiquities. Someone had definitely hidden away at one time, probably illegally gained.   It was never established to be from one particular region. Without any proper records or documentation coming forward, she was allowed to keep a huge share of it. She was about your age at the time. We were fixing over the house, and well, you know how kids can be. Finding that treasure was truly wonderful and it saved our family, but it also came at a price for Mary. You must know how hard it is to stand out."

I put my head down, even though it is dark. My face burns from being flushed. I can't even imagine. How much crap the kids must have given her. "She took a lot of teasing from the kids at school. A lot of people, not just the children, accused her of stealing it. That was hard for her. Then when she was a bit older, she married Declan's father, and ..." I can tell she is trying to season what she says, trying not to reveal too much.

Trying to smooth over any possible information Grandma might have given or mistakenly screwed up.

She starts again, "Anyway, that didn't work out so well...and then she left." I try to think of the most mature thing I can say, " That's a bummer," Is all that comes to mind. She smiles, "Yes, it is most definitely a bummer." She drops me at the back glass doors.

I can see my father rummaging around the kitchen, probably fixing himself an unhealthy snack. At one time this would have seemed like such a major offense. Now after the last couple of days, it seems so silly. It is a nice feeling to see him, just your average guy. No dark secrets, or hidden drama. Being ordinary and mildly dull never looked so inviting as it does now.

I wish Deidre goodnight. Turning to go inside, I fight back the urge to hug her. After I see her shadow against the moonlight, a dark shadow walking alone across the field. I wish I had hugged her. I like this family. I am glad my parents have brought me to Ireland. I am glad this family has taken me in, even if it is for only one evening.

It is amazing how my father stays thin, the way he loves to hit the snacks before bed. He is not too particular on what he has, so long as it is junky. He drives my mother crazy, she must have some sort of device attached to him. Within minutes of him piling a plate of food, she enters and pounces on him. "Oh, Jack, how could you, after that gorgeous meal we had tonight?" He shrugs his shoulders sheepishly and then looks over towards me for support. My mom follows his gaze, "Oh hi sweetie, I didn't know you were back, how was your evening with Anna?" I smile towards Dad, I am glad I can take the heat off him, if only for a while. We talk for a few minutes, all of us nibbling chips off my father's plate.

I watch my parents, realizing I should be grateful for the averageness of Jack and Kelly. I probably should even be a little more understanding of my father losing his job. I took it so personally, as if I was the only one who was affected by it. They are nice people, and they do put me first. I really have it pretty good. I am going to cut them more leeway in the future. Or at least try.

We say our goodnights and my parents casually head for bed, while I stand at the landing, looking up the dark staircase towards my room. I am reluctant to go to bed. Who am I kidding; I am afraid to go to bed. I am not really sure why. It is not that I had a bad dream. I mean technically I haven't had a nightmare. More I am frightened by the feelings I feel after waking up from my dreams. The panic, the terror, the fear, is that something scary is going to happen. I try to rationalize my feelings, if this even makes sense. I am confused. I am starting to give myself a headache. I brush my teeth, turn off the bathroom light, and head up the last set of steps.

Lying in bed I listen to the wind. In typical Ireland fashion it quickly turns gale force. I can tell by the flying debris hitting the roof with sporadic thumps. Here the houses are made out of concrete block, so while the wind outside is ripping off limbs and shearing trees of leaves, inside, it sounds like a blustering breeze. With just the occasional tap of something hitting it's actually kind of soothing. Having so little sleep the night before, it's not long before the noise lulls me to sleep.

Chapter 8

Waking up early from a dreamless night. At least I think it was dreamless. I feel a sense of urgency to get into town and visit with the seal. Which is strange, because I should be more interested in getting up to the castle. One thing I am certain of with these cryptic dreams, there is a connection to Lady Vivian. I need to get up there and poke around more.

The difference at the harbor is apparent as soon as I step foot on the small stone bridge. It's not just the smell of diesel and the loud engines. The tranquil little cove atmosphere has transformed into a bustling tourist marina. Huge cabin cruisers and sailboats flying flags from all over Europe form what looks to be a parade of vessels entering.

People emerge from the hatches below to wave or stretch in preparation to dock. Each boat trawls slowly along in single file. Like the Rose Bowl Parade, boats float one behind the other, in an orderly fashion. Sludge and seaweed spit out the back end through the tailpipes. Engines on the larger boats let off a protested purr, the only way to show their objection to being tamed, put in low gear, made to slow and eventually stop, after grappling the huge waves outside the channels. Their reluctance to slow is because it goes against the nature of their design; they are built to command the ocean waters, slicing through the menacing huge waves.

The tiny metal cleats attached to the temporary docks are all filled. The bright colored buoys in the middle of the basin are all spoken for, as well. The smaller crafts are tied on and buck and turn with the wake of waves made by the traffic. I am amazed at how many new boats have arrived since I was last here.

Boats that had there fill of dry land and the village life head out, forming another lane of traffic. Crews made up of families, or friends try to keep order as they join the slow group moving into the lane of traffic that will eventually spread and open to the sea. Although these crews are mostly made of families and recreational boaters, there is an experience and expertise among all. Each person has an important job, and it is of the utmost importance they execute it safely. The youngest passengers remain seated with bright life vests; they carry an understanding not to get in the way.

A large man gracefully jumps from the main dock onto the temporary metal ones. He does this every few minutes. A crew needs help, either parking their vessels, or beginning to cast off. Ropes of all sizes and widths are thrown towards him. His arms swell and colossal muscles flex taught, resembling roots from some ancient tree. At times, he single-handedly orchestrates the safe docking of a boat bigger than an armored truck. Pulling the ropes like a puppet master, the craft does a last shimmy before it gives in to his brute strength and will.

Large rubber bumpers are dropped between the boat and the dock to keep from scraping the sides. The powerful engine is turned off and the boat seems to sink a little in the water. The blades from the engine take a last few more violent turns before silently they relent and quietly give in. The last of the ocean bilge secretes out the back, discoloring the white froth left from the engine blades. The man pushes other boats away from the dock, quickly collecting the ropes and tossing them to the people aboard. Waving them towards the lane of traffic that will lead back to the ocean. Moving them sometimes in haste, to make way for another boat, who is present and waiting to grab the vacant dock.

Fishing boats, buoy boats, and sailboats moored in the small inlet shake and quake from all the movement brought in by the traffic. The water swells and sprays up on to the tiny wall and farther still onto the footpath. Locals know enough to avoid walking on that side of the street. Anna joins the rest of the children in their bright colored rain slickers and wellie boots as they race to use that particular sidewalk. She takes one last romp in the puddles and overspray before we cross the street and head into the library.

After my usual errands, I find a comfortable dry spot on the wall. I begin unwrapping the familiar brown paper, looking for my fish carcass. I notice I have quite a few extra pieces and I begin littering the murky water with them. A silver shadow begins gobbling the pieces. The seal grabs the fish in a more greedy way than in the past. He is agitated, and darts back and forth, never resting in one particular place too long. After binging on all the food I have to offer and giving one great leap, the seal disappears.

Feeling the heat of a stare, I glance up. The man with the huge arms is glaring at me. Perched like a hawk on one of the temporary docks. I see him take flight, heading up the makeshift stairs. He looks pretty angry about something. That must be the Sea Captain. He certainly seems to be in command of the busy flow of boats.

Whoever he is, he has quite an intimidating presence. If I didn't know better I would have said he was heading my direction. Before he can get any closer, I hear the sound of metal scrapping against metal. He turns around in enough time to catch a cabin cruiser scrapping along the side of the dock. The metal along the side of the boat makes what sounds to be a high - pitched scream. The speed and weight causes a small spray of sparks. A thin slice of the boat rolls backwards into what looks like a gigantic carrot peel. He abruptly changes directions, and heads towards the accident.

Anna steps up behind me, without uttering a word. "Hey kid, how was your day?" I smile cheerfully. She usually waits for me at the library, so I am a little startled at seeing her cross the road. She mumbles something inaudible, and heads towards the bridge leading home. Her boots land heavy on the cobblestones, as if she picked up some extra weight. "Are you okay?" I don't normally ask when she is in a quiet mood. I know she has a lot on her mind. But today, I can sense something bigger, something is truly bothering her. "No bother, Audrey. You want to take a walk later," she asks. I know what Anna's walks mean. She wants to head up to the castle and scan the sea for her father. "Yeah, no problem," I agree with her. I am not looking forward to the strenuous hike to get there, but I have my own business to take care of at the castle.

Over my shoulder, I see Tim Fielding, the little creep that was teasing Anna up on the path at the castle. He is exiting the library and I have a sneaking suspension he may be behind Anna's heavy heart. She was in a great mood when I dropped her. That little jerk probably said something hurtful. I wait till I am sure Anna's back is to me, and then I turn slightly and let out my best impression of a crow. He quickly ducks his head, closing his eyes. Anna turns, also scared by the loud sound I made. She looks over to see Timmy a look of complete terror on his face, peering up to the sky to see if the raven is back. His mother grabs a hold of his chubby little hand and heads in the opposite direction. This puts a slight smile on Anna's face, not enough to change her mood, but enough to help a little.

After a quick lunch, I wash my face, about to apply sunscreen. I push air through my cheeks as I look at my face. My cheeks seem so fat to me. My nose slightly crooked. Adults, mostly my mother's friends, will often comment on my looks. They say I have my mother's high cheekbones. They comment on how lucky I am, that it is such an asset. I don't see it. I see a geeky, teenager looking back at me. Applying the cream may be a little bit over the top, the chance we will have a full day of sun is pretty much hopeless. I pull my face close to the mirror. I see this "oil-free" sunscreen has in fact, left a dime size residue of oil on my hand. If not careful I could have a major blow out of zits. I will definitely need a major cleanse later. I still don't want the alternative of not using sunscreen, being a wrinkled old prune at the age of twenty. A vision I see one to many of at the beaches back home. I prefer an even tan that comes in a tube, or a spray. Besides that, my pale skin always burns, and then peels. Most times there is no tan at all. This is Ireland, what am I thinking. Even on a continually bright day there is not exactly tropical rays with all the clouds around.

We stop at the end of the driveway, behind the tiny red strand of yarn, and wait. It is amazing that having a herd of cows cross in front of me with the only barrier being this tiny yarn, has actually become kind of commonplace. We smile and wave as the Kennedy clan follows behind the herd.

Anna walks a pace behind me, trying to act as if nothing is bothering her. I know her well enough by now to see through it. She hasn't said three words since leaving the library.

The walk up the side of the mountain seems easier today. Both of us so lost in our own thoughts. We barely notice the steady incline. As we near the castle, I stop at the ruins. Anna hurries ahead. Today will be one of her quiet days. She will spend what will seem like hours just looking out to sea. She won't need my company for now.

Standing in the middle of where the Great Hall stood allows me enough distance to take in one side of the ruins. My imagination works, putting the pieces of the castle back together. I can see the layout plain and clear. I know now this is where my dreams take me. I have been here. It once stood unbroken and I was here then.

The dream from yesterday is fresh in my mind. I walk the tall unkempt grass that grows, where the rooms once stood. I can see the hallway and feel the warmth from the torch. It is so peculiar to have your mind fill in the gaps and crevices, to rebuild the castle that lies in twisted rocks what is now a cow pasture. I move around what once was a hallway. I am so comfortable and familiar in this strange place. Entering what was the kitchen, I step where the long thick wood table stood. The herbs hung over the fireplace, the smell of something hardy cooking. It all comes flooding back.

The woman from my dream, I know her. We are connected. Her long dark thick hair, she is not a stranger. Her voice is so familiar. So much like family.

A moment of clarity rushes me. I awake from the trance that has held me here in these ruins. I am left here in the present, in the fields, littered with memories. Moments ago, it was a fully functioning, fully intact medieval castle.

I remind myself of something I already know. In those dreams, there is someone else that I know, that I am comfortable with and can trust. Someone is trying to send me a message. But what is the message? Who needs my help? That is what I need to find out.

Could it be Anna? Maybe Anna needs me? I rush through the walled old garden, stumbling on rocks and rubble as I go. The cows leisurely walk in front of my path and I push at them. I round the small stonewall. I am about to call out. When I see her, I mean I really see her. She is sitting completely still and stoic, like a statue. On her face is sadness. A solitary tear falls down a worn path. She is not up here to wait for her father. Her face tells the real story. She is up here to let her father pass. She is accepting the pain of her loss in small doses. She sits on that path, in that same spot she always sits at, and she regulates her grief. It doesn't define her. Rather it is something she has chosen to manage. Our trips to the castle are when she releases it, a bit at a time. She suffers in silence, in these small self-appointed moments. She allows the truth, the fact that her father is not coming back, to slowly seep in. In reflective moments that she chooses, high up here on these peaceful cliffs, she is coming to terms with the inevitable. She is here to say good-bye.

She senses my presence, and I quietly sit down next to her, grabbing her hand. I give a slight squeeze. Her honey colored eyes flood with tears that spill down her small white cheeks. I brush back the little tight curls that have stuck to her wet face. She turns her face back to the sea. I look out in the other direction allowing her the dignity of quiet sorrow. I am in awe; I have such a respect for this young girl. How clever of her, to come and expel her emotions in this magnificent place. This plot we share with the ghosts who are living, as well as those long dead. My feelings for her have grown and changed. I now feel such admiration and love for her resilience and inner strength. To think, when I first met her, I thought her a small silly child. I was dreading the thought of having to spend my summer with her tagging along cramping my style. How wrong I was. I gently run my hands through her hair, apologizing to her in my mind. I offer her my silent support. I value her decision, to do this on her own terms. I will stay next to her. I will quietly stand guard over her pain for as long as she needs me. I let her mourn alone, uninterrupted.

I have never sat down next to someone for such a long time without feeling the need to have some sort of conversation. A requirement felt to fill the empty void, mostly with mindless chatter. It is incredibly peaceful to sit here and not utter a word.

From this spectacular vantage point, I watch the huge tankers travel the international waterways, each carrying their own special cargo. Massive vessels travel silently miles below me. Each tanker must be at least the size of my football field at school. Flags and painted insignia travel the sea below from as far away as Russia and China. Proudly, they fly high above on masts as tall as skyscrapers.

Judging from the sun, we must have been sitting here for at least an hour or two, and still we have hardly said a handful of words. Anna turns and smiles at me. Her tears dry, the thin trail of moisture on her cheeks has long evaporated.

She looks as if she is about to say something. I lean over and hug her. I don't need her to explain anything. Our closeness speaks enough words to fill volumes. I stand and brush the loose dirt from the back of my pants, and extend my hand for her to follow.

As we head towards the road, her sadness is less. For now she puts it back on the imaginary shelf, until the next time she is ready to handle it. It is a shame she doesn't teach her mother Deidre this trick.

Deidre wears her pain on her face, sort of set on her jaw. It is always present, always ready. We pass the castle ruins and I nod. I am grateful for this deeper understanding with Anna. If that is whom I am here to help, I have no problem. I look up at the ravens that have begun circling the tall walls of what was once the castle atrium. I almost say it aloud, and then looking back, I make sure Anna isn't aware of my thoughts. She is still containing her grief, oblivious to me. I get the message. I am here for her. I will cover Anna with a bevy of love and support while she grieves.

Chapter 9

Taking a long shower doesn't seem to help to wash off the concern for Anna, or the whole castle, hocus pocus stuff. I will use Anna's tactics and put all this concern away on a shelf. I don't want to carry it around with me now.

Throwing my head back, I twist my wet hair in a towel. No need to wipe the steam off this mirror. The European immersion tanks heat up the water as needed, and only in small portions, preventing me from my hour shower with the water so hot it pinks my skin. I am lucky to get five minutes of hot water, any longer, and the rest of the house has cold water for the night. I dress casually in a purple turtle neck sweater and faded jeans. I give myself a good long once over in the big mirror in the hallway, and for a change, I like what I see. I head down the small flight of stairs toward the kitchen and stop just long enough to grab a carrot stick and Dad's laptop. "Hurry up Audrey, your father is changing, then we are heading into town for trivia night."

I am feeling so confident tonight, strong enough to check my messages. I guess I have to take some responsibility for not receiving any messages. I mean I was so upset no one wrote me, but I didn't write anyone either. So I guess some of the burden of responsibility falls on me. I know what kind of work goes into keeping up a popularity status. I have fallen way behind. I will need to do a lot of butt kissing and general sucking up just to get back to the level I was at when I left. Not to mention, how much new ground that has been lost, since I haven't been on-line daily. At everyone's beck and call, to capture every moment, in the instant it occurs.

I decide to send out a general WHA-UP? Then I will see who bites back. I am about to hit send all, when I stop. My hand freezes. My friend's only real concern is how many texts they have, not who they are from, or what the sender may have on their mind. They just want dirt, gossip, a reason to bash someone, so they feel better about themselves. Half these kids only allegiance, only friendship is with drama. Anything else is just far too threatening to their fragile ego to be loyal or faithful too.

The computer asks if I want to save my message, I decline. Instead making a promise to myself. Next year, I will find a friend who is credible and worthy. Someone I actually care about what they think, and in return they will care about my opinions. It won't be anyone using me to get his or her own popularity numbers up.

I won't burn any bridges by being self-righteous, or anything that stupid. I am not ready to commit social suicide. But I will be on the lookout for something better. I hear my mother's voice. I shout back curtly, "I am coming." I turn my back on the faint green hue that fills the darkened room as the computer slowly shuts itself off.

Allowing my mother to put my hair up in a loose twist in the back brings her instant pleasure. What the heck, it is super frizzy weather out there. I can hear my father whistling while he shaves. Wow it has been a long time since I have seen or heard him even remotely happy. I grab a number of cans of tuna, and open them. Dumping all the contents into a plastic container, I smash the lid down tightly. Before rinsing out the empty cans burying them in the recycling. Washing my hands swiftly, I am at the front door before my parents are even aware. We crunch along the stone drive and head towards the car. My parents have to switch positions. Once again they have forgotten which side of the car has the steering wheel on it. They give each other an embarrassed laugh, and we head into the village. "I don't know when the last time we went out together as a family," my father asks proudly.

We pull into the one parking lot the entire village shares. There are a lot of people milling around but the lot is almost empty. So many people arrive here via the sea.

I see Aunt Carol and her husband closing up the fish shop. I give a wave and a long stare. I wonder, who is Carl's sibling? Maybe he was getting fish for them, when the accident occurred. They don't seem as affected by the whole thing as Deidre and Anna. Grandma definitely would have mentioned the fish shop. I may have been asleep by that point.

Some kids are hanging around near the library, so I seize the opportunity to have an alibi. "I want to head over and say hello, then I will meet you guys inside." My parents nod and I note that the pub is right there. I will join them shortly. I wave them on and head towards the group. Waiting for my parents to enter, and head out of sight. I cross the street and head to the side of the wall that runs along the water. I have no idea who those kids are and they soon walk off in the other direction.

Shaking my head, I am not sure why I haven't shared the seal stuff with them. I guess old habits die-hard. One of these days, I will tell them the whole sordid story. I drop my bag and grab the plastic container. After wrestling with the top, I finally pry it open. The pungent aroma of canned tuna fills the night air as I sit with my feet dangling over the side. After throwing a few pieces I wait. I know this isn't the usual time I feed them, but the seal seemed really hungry earlier. Maybe, all the excitement of the boats in the area is preventing him from surfacing. I toss some more out, a bit farther. This causes some movement; a small head creeps up beneath my feet and grabs a small piece. In the distance a boat engines turns on, and the seal darts back under. I am just about to throw another piece when a shadow passes over me, covering the last of the early evening sun.

"Just what do you think you are doing?" A voice growls at me. I look up to see the man with the tremendous arms, from the harbor glaring down at me. I have to squint in the evening light to see him.

Jumping up while kicking the plastic container over the side into the water allows varying size pieces of tuna to strewn the water and float around just below us. The plastic bobs for just a second before it fills with water and slowly sinks.

I am frozen in fear. He grabs my arm. A radiant pain shoots all the way to my shoulder. I get a clear smell of his sweaty body odor mixed with the stink of stale whiskey. "Nothing, I was just... I mean I was..." At a complete lack of words, my heart pounds so fast, I am certain it will explode out of my chest. Nope, instead, it has decided to lodge itself in my throat.

"You foolish girl, have you no sense?" His thick dark eyebrows narrow as he spits his words at me. "Are you trying to set a trap to kill some poor seal?" He points to the engine that is being lifted from a boat, the blades turn slicing and chopping pieces of seaweed with incredible precision. "How do you expect your friend to get out of here with a million of those in the water? I don't know whether you noticed or not, but I got a harbor full of those engines that are attached to some pretty big machinery. Have you figured out how you expect your little friend will fair in that? I think he may well be chopped up six different ways to Sunday.

If he isn't run down first, all thanks to you." I hear him mutter, "stupid," as he finally lets go of my arm.

My eyes fill with tears, which spill over and begin pouring down my cheeks. "I am here, for the summer I am staying ....with...a...Anna Byrne." I am terrified. I can barely speak.

This seems to fuel his anger more, and he moves in closer, grabbing my arm again. He squeezes even tighter. "I don't give a flying fig how you got in me harbor. You are playing a very dangerous game."

The humiliations of his tone and his angry words, plus the pain in my arm, are nothing compared to the realization of what he is saying. No matter what kind of mean monster he is. He is right, and that is truly painful.

It never even dawned on me that I was baiting the seal. Training him to stay in the harbor and look for food. I had no idea that the cove would fill with so many boats, so much traffic. Now it is extremely dangerous with all the engines. How will he ever get out? What have I done? My head is swirling and the pressure on my arm is throbbing.

Someone behind lets out an indignant shout, "Davis, what are you doing?" He turns towards the voice and squints his eyes blinded by a last blast of the sun. "Mary, is that you?" His voice suddenly takes on a new tone. Now it sounds hopeful and vulnerable. I turn to see the silhouette, it is Deidre and she is holding a small persons hand. I assume its Anna.

I am also blinded by the sun, and can only make out their outline. The man drops my arm. "Did you see what she has been doing?" This time his voice is not as vulnerable but still shaky. He is definitely flustered. Deidre moves in, "She is a child, for heavens' sake. She has no idea. She mean's no harm." I have never seen this side of Deidre. She is strong and set in her conviction. She stands and stares with complete hatred. She really does not like this man, and it is obvious.

He scowls at Deidre and adds, "You don't know what she is doing here. She is daft. Just cause you don't like me, you can't deny that this is wrong. If that seal gets caught in an engine it won't just kill the seal. I have a harbor to look after."

Deidre turns a cold shoulder to him. She speaks to the man, but her body is turned away looking out to sea. Reluctant to speak and a little nervous almost, she takes a breath and begins. "Its not what you're saying Davis, it's how you go about it. You can't just bully the world. You have to stop taking out your anger on everyone who is here. She isn't coming back to you. Mary is gone. You need to let it rest. You owe it to all of us." She waits before adding, "especially Declan." At the mention of Declan's name, the old man straightens up and tenses. Deidre has obviously hit a nerve with this cold man.

A figure appears behind, "McMahon, Captain McMahon, that boat is arriving. Do you want to come over?" We all look up, grateful to the stranger for the distraction. "Ya, I am coming." He shoots me one last black look before he brushes past me. Following the man who has unknowingly diffused live ammunition that is ready to misfire.

My arm burns as I try to rub away the pain. I have been publicly humiliated, as well as had the circulation squeezed out of my arm. I realize I got off easy when I look at the shock that is clearly evident on Deidre's face. "Are you okay?" I end up asking her.

She turns towards me, her facial expression is different, and a small smile forms on her face. "I have wanted to say something to that man for, I don't know how long. It feels great." She turns towards Anna, who stands still as a statue. Deidre and Anna look to me at the same moment, "Are you okay luv? Anna and I have seen how cruel he can be, especially when he directs his anger straight at ya." I can tell there is a lot of unresolved baggage left. I decide to try to act casual and brush it off. We head up the stairs and towards the pub.

"Don't you give that man and his evilness a second thought. Seals, every once in a while come into the harbors. The water is warmer and shallow and they can feed on smaller fish. That has been happening since I was a wee girl. You certainly aren't the first person to feed them. Davis McMahon is a mean spirited, bull-headed man. He is a big part of the reason my sister left this village. When she was married to him, she was miserable. He was a tyrant, and he...." She pauses for a moment, realizes whom she is speaking to. She looks to be wondering if she has said too much. She abruptly stops. "I am sorry girls for the ugly events. Look here, it's a beautiful evening. Lets try to enjoy the rest of it, shall we?"

It is a spectacular night. The sky over the water is turning a gorgeous pink, and the huge clouds look almost silver. The water has taken on the hues from the sky and pompously reflects them back. The last of the sunlight bursts in between the clouds, to light the way.

We walk across the cobblestones towards the pub. Many of the boats have twinkly Christmas lights strung to them, and they slowly begin to turn on. People stroll leisurely past us with no particular destination. Smiling and chatty, they are in a tourist traveling mode. It is hard to let the ugly events of a few moments earlier linger. I came out tonight to enjoy myself, with my parents. I am not going to let some mean old guy bring me down. Deidre has made me feel a lot better. I just gave the seal some small treats. I am not the criminal that man is trying to make me out to be.

Anna swings open the pub door, and the warmth as well as the soft Irish music pulls me inside. The pub is crowded, each table filled with families of all ages laughing and joking. There are teenagers conversing with what looks to be their grandparents, and in public, for that matter. I am blown away. My parents have found a small booth next to Anna's family. I see Aunt Carol from the fish shop sitting with Grandma. My face breaks into an enormous smile, feeling so much better and truly safe, with my parents, Deidre, Grandma, and Anna. My mother looks up her face flashing a look of concern at me. She stares behind my transparent smile.

Our dark wood table is small, the carpet beneath dark blue with a gold leaf diamond pattern running through. It lets off a stale odor of beer. There are two small three legged stools. My parents are sharing the booth. I pick the stool on the opposite side, positioning myself between the two tables, trying not to make too much eye contact with my mom. The waitress comes by to offer us a sticky plastic menu and a half sheet of paper with a broken pencil. Engrossing myself in reading does nothing to feign off my mothers intrusive eye. "If you be wanting to eat, you be best to put in your order now. As soon as the questions start, the kitchen will close." The waitress announces before she waddles off to the next table to repeat the message.

I look down to see the same offerings listed as on every other pub menu. Fish and chips, soup, shepherds pie, sausage and chips. I order the fish and chips. I know better than to think chips, mean potato chips. I have found that out the hard way. Anna orders a packet of crisps with her fish. Which means a bag of potato chips.

Declan steps into the pub. He is with Davis. I realize that awful man, who berated me outside, is his father. I didn't want to make the connection, but seeing them now together is proof. I am surprised at how much they look alike. I see his weather beaten face is still stern and intimidating. His face has wrinkles that crease and set a match to his hard expression. He whispers something to Declan and then turns and heads to the bar.

Declan crosses over and comes to stand in front of our table. I smile and gesture towards the empty stool. He nods before dropping his hat at our table and then excuses himself to wash up in the bathroom.

I am more than a little afraid of his father. What if he notices me sitting at a table with his son? I glance across the table at my parents. I don't think that he will start any more trouble with my parents here. I see Deidre looking over at him. She still looks visibly shaken by their run in. I doubt he will want to tangle with her again.

While Declan is gone, our food arrives. The waitress brings a steaming bowl of soup, a crust of bread, and an orange soda. Setting it down in front of the chair that Declan has left his hat on.

Declan returns with his hands and arms clean. His clothes look as if he has had a full day at the soot yard. He at least has made an obvious effort to pat off the loose dirt, leaving only a few stains. He immediately starts in on his food. A silent understanding that it was put there for him. I can tell he must be a regular guest.

Every table is filled with families. All the members in groups have similar features. Some faces splotched slightly red from those who work the sea. Some hands are worn, from those who work the land. There is a trust, a bond of sorts. Everyone pulls his or her weight. I see the butcher and his family, the doctor and his. I feel as if I am in a time warp, back to what I would imagine was an easier time.

The trivia game begins. The man behind the huge mahogany bar shouts out a question. Families huddle together to come to an answer. Declan and my parents jump right in, tossing ideas, and whispering answers. Someone picks up the broken pencil and jots it down on the scrap of paper.

I am trying to have an interest in the questions the barman is asking, but I am drawn towards Captain McMahon. He is a truly frightening man. He reminds me of some of the teachers in middle school. They wander around the hallways just looking to bust you on any infraction they can find. "Do you have a hall pass? Is that gum in your mouth?" It is as if yelling at you or humiliating you in any possible way will somehow make up for how bad they feel inside. We as students are easy targets, sitting ducks. If we try to defend ourselves against their unprovoked attacks, then we end up being considered a disciplinary problem, resulting in even more trouble. Its better to just take your lumps, and keep your mouth shut.

After meeting Captain McMahon I now know miserable adults who try to get a little pleasure in their unhappy lives by bringing down kids is a worldwide epidemic.

Although this was a bit more than the average yelling, he grabbed my arm and hurt me. There is a dull throb where each of his fingers burrowed into my skin, and the rage and anger in his voice, it was more than just your less than satisfied with middle-age life adult.

I watch the Captain through the bar mirror. He makes himself comfortable at the corner barstool. He hasn't even bothered to look up at the people in the dining room, or to check if his son is okay. He seems very familiar with that spot. Perched on his high backed fabric red mahogany barstool. He is slightly hunched over in front of a steaming bowl of soup, accompanied by a huge glass of dark beer with large foam.

His features are so similar to Declan's. I get rare glimpses of the front of his face from the mirror that is across from him, attached to the back railings of the bar.

His skin is worn and tanned. Like a fisherman's would be but his, holds even more age to it. He appears to be a worn out and extremely angry version of Declan. I can see why Deidre thinks so little of him. I am still pretty shaken up about the altercation with him. I try to blame the whole thing on his obvious messed up mentality. Deep down I know the truth. In his angry and ugly way, he had a point.

My mother can read the worry on my face. She looks up from her wonderful evening with a concerned look and mouths, "Are you okay?" I smile my pretend smile and assure her I am great. I am not about to burden her tonight.

I am watching how much fun they are having and it is long overdue. They have let a lot of the stress from the last year lift and now are visibly lighter. It has been a long time since we had an evening like this. It is nice to see them laugh and joke.

Working together as a team makes the trivia game intense. We are able to answer most of the questions. Almost all the Irish history questions being answered by Declan. He waits to make sure no one else is going to answer, before he offers up his guess. He is smart, yet doesn't flaunt it at all. He doesn't attract attention, preferring to stay quiet and reserved.

At the end, when all ten questions have been answered, the bartender comes out from behind the bar. The floor behind the mahogany block is raised on a platform, giving him an added height, which quickly diminishes. Standing on this side makes it apparent how truly short he is. His height almost matches his width, giving his figure roundness, like a beach ball. His stout frame further exaggerated by the small apron, bound tightly around his middle, stretching and pulling. It barely makes it around his waist. Being the keeper of the answers to the trivia game gives him an added stature. He is aware of this and lets the moment linger, basking in the glory for all it is worth.

The end of the game is the most fun. The bartender reads the answers and the family's respond with either a clap of excitement or a hiss, all in good fun. The room quiets and guests begin to gather their things and leave.

Deidre and Declan chat quietly with each other, occasionally looking towards me. Oh great, I bet she is telling Declan what happened on the pier with my run-in with his father. What do I care? His father is a psycho. Declan must know this by now. I feel my face heat as I turn away. The last thing I need is for either of these two to think I care, what some old guy thinks.

We are the last few customers. My parents begin to gather themselves making a move towards the door. Declan remains fixed in his stool.

"Are you okay," he asks with a little difficulty. "I guess you heard about what happened with your Dad?" I ask meekly. He answers first with a smile and nod. "Audrey, you are one of many who has had a run in with my father." He runs a nervous hand through his hair, before continuing, " I have had my share myself. Listen, its no bother to clear the harbor of a seal. I have done it loads of times. If you like I can help?" My parents stand behind me now, an indication they are ready to leave. I thank him for his offer and tell him I will see him tomorrow when I drop Anna in town. I glance back to see the waitress bring him a fresh soda. She walks over to the dusty ancient television that is bracketed to the wall and the ceiling. It sputters as she clicks it on.

We step out of the warmth of the pub. The evening has changed. A cold wind slaps at our faces. A completely different evening then the night we entered just a few hours ago. A cold wet rain moves over us in gusts. My mother fumbles to pull her over sized hood up. We linger in front of the picture window. I look back through the glass to see the bartender placing another pint, this time with a small shot glass in front of Captain McMahon. The waitress in the room next door finishes cleaning the abandoned tables, as Declan stretches out in the booth. The one my parents just occupied. He has the room to himself as he becomes engrossed with something on the old screen. Obviously, this is a familiar evening for Declan.

Chapter 10

It is a wonder I can sleep at all, the Captain's cruel words continually ringing in my head. Tossing and turning, my body unable to relax while my mind imagines one gruesome accident after another. The small gray body of the seal is being sucked under an engine, or worse. The helpless animal lets out a small cry, before being pulled under the water.

Sleep wins once again; the awful images of the seal subside. Tonight's dream starts in the castle. Down the spiral stone narrow staircase, I stop to look out the small rectangle window. The ship is still far out to sea. The huge white masts billow in the wind. The dark wood hull moves gracefully as it cuts through the enormous waves. I continue down the windy stairs. My breath becomes quicker with each step. Panic builds. My heart is pounding so hard. I turn the corner into a great room. The heads of the animals she has slain are affixed to the walls. She is an incredible hunter.

It is hard to believe they were killed, now dead and mounted. She is fanatical about making them as real in death as they were in life. Methodically, she paints each glass eye that now stares back at me. Their expressions look as ferrous in death as they did before they were killed. Their fur is neatly combed. Each hair lies together in perfect harmony.

The worst is when the first arrow doesn't quite kill them. They need to be finished off. She expertly uses the knife to do the job. Before they are hung and drained of blood. The entire lot of inside organs fed to those disgusting ravens that follow her every step.

Passing through the kitchen, I see that the fire will need fresh wood. I must hurry because the boat is coming. It is my job to keep the kitchen fire burning and I have fallen behind. I run through the back around the corner jumping the wall. I know to scoop up my long dress, so it doesn't catch on the brambles and thorns. I quickly collect some smaller twigs and branches. I place these next to the hearth, before heading to the woodpile, to grab some of the larger logs.

I begin to add the larger logs to the smoldering red and black coals. I steady my shaking hand, carefully placing each small branch and log into a triangle formation. This will allow the air to pass through the middle and maximize the heat and flame. I quickly add some kindling to the top and lean in to blow on the fresh new embers. No matter what happens to us tonight, this fire will burn. I take a moment to stare into the flames, "I hope to see you later." I give a small respectful bow.

Fire represents a continued future. I know how important those small flames are, it is crucial for me to care for them. A pinch in my lower back as I straighten it, makes me stand a little slower, allowing me to glance out through the kitchen door.

A shape cloaked in a dark wrap moves up the path towards the garden. Her black hair flows loosely. She is smiling at me. Her light blue dress is slightly soiled and worn. The lace around the bodice has slightly discolored. It takes a keen eye to see it is beginning to yellow. Around her neck, completely out of place with the rest of her appearance, lies a sparkling sapphire necklace. Each luminous stone the size of a walnut set in solid silver that glimmers with each step. The last reminder of the life that once lived inside these castle walls.

"Are the lanterns ready?" She asks. Her beautiful green eyes show no sign of fear. She passes me to grab a large, crudely made basket that waits just beside the wall. Placing some of the twigs that have broken free from the tight braid back through the weave. She instantly makes the worn basket look almost new again.

"Come we can pick something to put in a tart." I stop in my tracks, "A tart, did you say a tart? The death boats are coming." I am so afraid, words spit out of my mouth as I speak. She slowly looks towards the sea. A harsh cold look crosses over her face. Then it turns completely emotionless.

"Not tonight, they won't. There is a storm coming, I can smell it." She breathes deep; looking up at the clear, quiet evening sky. "Those savages have no idea how to maneuver against our rain and gale winds. Their tropical storms are child's play compared to what they will see tonight. There will be no collection of our people tonight, mind you. But tomorrow we will find many of those scaly wags. They will be dead from the merciless sea and we will be the better for it." She lets out a terrible cackle, a dark laugh. The cold heartless stare that has possessed her face now passes.

She turns gentle again, happy, almost child - like. "Come let us prepare for a tart." I feel a coldness run through my body. I fear not for the death ships that wait outside just beneath the horizon, vessels that come and take our people. My fear is for her. Her mind is touched. The horrific ordeal she has lived through has seared her. Scarred her inside.

Her voice takes on almost a singsong rhyme as she skips down the path. "How long has it been since we have had a real dessert?"

She is so proud, "That is right, I have bargained for some ground meal, so tonight we shall have a tart with our supper." I stop in my tracks before asking, "You traded for wheat? From whom did you trade, and where? Did you allow them in the castle?" She twirls around gracefully. The precious stones from her necklace catch in the last of the evening sun sending a sparkling reflection across the garden.

She smiles before answering, "Of course not my darling girl, I would never be that careless. I traded with the blacksmith from the village. He is allowed out of the walled city to work on the horses that travel for supplies. I met him on the other side of the woods. He has no idea who I am."

A chill runs over me. "I don't know Mum. It seems awfully dangerous. You shouldn't have gone alone. You should have protection." We walk together through the garden, headed for the berry fields. "Oh, but I did my dear. Catherine Mary waited in the woods with her bow drawn."

The idea of Catherine with her bow drawn sends me into a fit of laughter. "Catherine Mary couldn't hit an ox cart from a pace away, even if it was stopped. Why, you're lucky she didn't end up shooting her own foot or worse yet, shooting you." This starts us both laughing. Vivian turns towards me, "You are right about that, the girl has a hopeless shot. The blacksmith says he would be willing to trade for a horse, if the metals were heavy enough."

This is a quandary indeed. To have a horse would be amazing. It would open up this land for miles. We would be free to hunt distant fields and travel to farther villages to trade our wares. But as I point out to Vivian, it leaves us vulnerable. It means someone would know us. We have spent our lives making sure we are left alone. Protecting ourselves: from the dangerous world that lies outside the wood line. To think we would do business with a person who lives behinds the gates of the village, and with the very soldiers we fear. It could be far too risky.

We will need to think about it. One thing is for certain. The next time she wants to be meeting up with this man, it will be with me guarding her in the woods. I will have my bow drawn and arrows ready to protect and defend.

After collecting a basket of the finest berries the patch has to offer, we enjoy a beautiful pheasant. Our beloved tart cools on the rack.

The raven screams. Vivian jumps from the table. "A stranger approaches. Girls quickly grab your weapons." We climb the stairs two at a time winding and twisting to the top of castle. The light from our torches flickers and sways with each step of the winding and treacherous stone stairs. We all work to keep our flame alive. Catherine swings open the hatch. The cool evening air has changed the night is misty. I look out over the sea. The last of the evening light illuminates our other enemies. The large boats far out on the horizon now rock and buckle more exaggerated than before, the wind begins to pick up and howl at my ears.

The ravens scream louder still. Vivian is crouched down squinting her eyes desperate to find the intruder, in the open fields below. She cries out in a voice barely recognizable. "I can seeeee youuuuuu." She is silent. She waits for a moment. She barks in a deep guttural voice, "I will give you but a moment to turn and go back, for if you take another step towards us, it will be followed with the last breath you will breathe on this earth." No response, no sound at all and too dark to get a visual. We begin to soak the tips of the arrows in the flammable liquid while we ready our bows. She turns and looks over her shoulder before she whispers, "I can't see them, help me my brave soldiers."

Over our heads the ravens fly. One lets out a cry long and steady. Vivian leans and aims directly below the bird's voice. The arrow lands barely hitting its mark. We hear a voice mutter and whimper, than the flame is rubbed out and the flammable liquid is spread.

Vivian turns towards me, "Freya, my dear, would you light the way for your mother?" I extend my bow and lean it slightly upwards. My arrow flies high and slowly glides through the sky sending a small torch of light. Vivian leans forward and aims. Her arrow flies straight and fast. A deadly stealth of flame pierces the dark night. There is a cry as the target realizes what is coming. The form bursts into flames.

Vivian waits for a moment craning to hear she waits for the ravens' response a long caaawwww. She leans her back to the castle wall and lets out a sigh of relief before asking in a quiet tone, "Catherine Mary would you please shoot out some light to make sure the fields are clear and in the name of your father extend your bow. I have a fresh tart that needs eating. I don't want to be spending the evening running around the castle putting out the fires from your missed shots."

A number of ravens land in and around us on top of the castle wall. They cry in short syllables. Agitated and angry they tap their beaks. Vivian slowly rises and looks out over the darkened fields. The last of the corpse burns as the rain begins to fall. "Oh dear, I am sorry me friends. I am afraid your dinner is burned this evening. Aaah but fear not, the rain will cool your meal. There should be some good pecking left." With that she slowly turns towards me and whispers. "You must help them still. They need you to help them. You must take care of them."

I open my eyes. Lying in the odd shaped blue bedroom on the top floor, I hear a crow. No it's not a crow. It is a raven.

Shaking the rest of the sleep from my head. The acrid smell of burning flesh is still fresh in my nostrils. My arm sore from extending to shoot the arrows, no, my arm is sore from where Captain McMahon grabbed it. There is something else. What or who is it that I am suppose to be taking care of? I am just a kid. I say it out loud, then again even louder. "I am just a kid, and I can barely take care of myself. What do you want from me?" I hear the cry of the bird, this time farther away, heading up the road behind the house on the path that leads to the castle. I am beginning to wonder if I should have ever gone up to that stupid castle ruins in the first place.

Chapter 11

I climb down the stairs, still going over every moment of my dream. I always have wild dreams when I eat preservatives. Either I had an incredible hit of additives in the fish and chips, or I am in serious trouble. I stumble into the kitchen trying to grapple the meaning of all of this. I enter the kitchen to see Anna and my mom sitting comfortably at the kitchen table. A fresh bowl of cereal with fruit on top sits in front of Anna. She grabs the spoon and dives in quickly.

My mother turns towards me "Honey, Deidre told me about the awful time you had with Declan's father. Is that Captain McMahon?" I glare over at Anna, Deidre's daughter. As if she could have kept her mother from blabbing. Anna puts her head towards her bowl of cereal, taking an over sized bite. She shrugs her shoulders as she makes a huge crunching sound. I recognize the lame attempt, looking as if she can't really respond with a mouthful of food.

To be honest, I don't know why I didn't tell my Mom about it last night. "Mom, I was going to say something to you. It just seemed like you and Dad were having such a good time. I didn't want to spoil it for you."

My mother looks over at me lovingly. "Oh sweetheart, that is so thoughtful of you. I just hate the idea of something bothering you, and you not feeling comfortable enough to share it with me. I am here to help you." It is funny, I am relieved Deidre told her. Normally something like this would have really bothered me. I am comfortable building a wall with my parents, not letting them see how I feel. But this time I am glad. I feel really uncomfortable having some nasty guy like Declan's father on my case. I know Deidre isn't terribly fond of the guy. She is on my side. But let's face it; with her trying to restart her career, she isn't exactly around a whole lot. I can't really count on a lot of back up from her. In fact, this was probably the only way she could feel like she was helping, to sort of recruit my mother to my cause.

"Honey, that guy sounds like a creep. If you want I will gladly go with you and give him a piece of my mind. So what, you threw some fish to a seal. Since when is that a federal crime?"

I love that about my Mom. When I really need her, she always has my back. "Okay Mom, I have to go to town today, so I will probably see him. I must admit I am a little bit afraid of what he might say. I don't think I need you to say anything, but I love the idea that you will be around town. Just in case he decides to start anymore crap."

That is all the prompting my mother needs, "Well don't worry honey. I have some shopping to do so I will head into town with you." The idea of my mother following my every move suddenly seems a little over the top. I don't think he is going to start any more trouble. I am feeling stronger today. I think I can handle this guy.

"Mom, I am okay, really. If you want we could meet up later? I can tell you how it went then." This seems to please her. I know I need to face this jerk and I need to do it alone. I am scared to see him again, if the truth were known. That fear will keep me from doing anything stupid. Like getting on the pier alone with him. Not after the last time. I am pretty sure she doesn't know about him grabbing my arm. That was pretty scary. "I am going to play it cool. I am not going to feed the seal or anything." As soon as the words come out of my mouth, I know they don't feel right. A nagging feeling rushes over me, an urgency to help. I have to feed the seal. I downplay my conviction to my mother and add casually, "I take that back, I am not going to feed the seals, where that guy can see me. I will be much more careful."

This last statement concerns her, and she furrows her eyebrows. "Please Audrey, promise me you will be. This guy sounds like a ticking time bomb." We agree.

Walking over the stone bridge, I scan the harbor to look for Captain McMahon. A rush of relief runs over me when I don't see him. I look over the other side of the bridge to the traveller's camp. There are a number of new camper trailers parked; a few more horses are tied close to the road munching hungrily at the tall grass that lines the sidewalk. I glance down at my reflection. It is hard to get a clear look at myself on this side of the bridge, because the water is much shallower and the rocks are scattered everywhere.

Ripples of waves travel under the bridge and break against the rocks, causing my image to duplicate itself. It is now as if I am standing next to a mirror image. I have to squint my eyes to try to see which one is the real me. I have to really focus. I spot the familiar torpedo shape of the seal. "Look Anna, he is on this side now." I turn towards the water, and speak directly to the seal. "You must have heard me getting chewed out last night. Listen, I will be back later. I will get you some fish, but I won't feed it to you, from the usual spot. I will feed you here, okay buddy?" Anna leans over and looks into the water and then looks back toward me. "You aren't waiting for him to answer, are you?"

She points to the library across the bridge on the other side of the marina. "Come on, I want to get a good pillow." She twirls me around and grabs my arm. The dull pain from where I held me bow and arrow...

I stop my thought from continuing. No, the dull pain from where Captain McMahon grabbed my arm last night is what I meant. The pang of pain breaks my playful mood. I race to keep up with her, rubbing away the dull throb all the while pushing back to the deep recess of my mind any thoughts of last nights dream.

Anna quickly finds a cushion and moves to a cozy spot. Giving it a solid punch, she sits down. I see through the tall glass Declan standing out front. He catches my eye and waves. Behind him, I can see in the distance, his father who is busy on the piers across the road.

I feel my nerves begin to fray. This is a small village, and I know I will be running into him. I just am not sure if I am ready this morning for too much drama. He looks busy enough. It is so awkward, I hate the idea of having to sneak around the old man constantly trying to avoid him. I take a deep breath and throw my shoulders back. I will be damned if I let that guy get under my skin. I pause a moment. He already is under my skin so let me rethink that. I will be damned if I let that guy know he has gotten to me. With that thought, I give another huge breath and blink hard as I open the glass doors that lead outside. "Hey Declan." I casually say trying to sound as calm as possible. I give a casual glance out of the corner of my eye at his father. He is absolutely oblivious to my presence.

Chapter 12

After a quick pit stop to pick up some fresh baked chocolate croissants, we stroll the stone road that separates the village from the harbor. We follow on land, the ancient stone jetties that lead out to sea. I am amazed to see that even more boats have jammed the tiny harbor since the night before. People emerge from below deck in many different phases of their morning routine. One man is holding a toothbrush, his face puffy from sleep. A woman climbs up from underneath a massive sailboat. She is dressed in a flowery skirt and straw hat. She gracefully maneuvers the small line metal rail that outlines her boat, jumping to the pier slightly below. Unfolding a canvas bag, she heads towards the open market. A man bids us good morning, heading towards the slip that holds his boat. A local newspaper tucked under his arm.

Passing the second set of piers, we hear the faint sound of a radio playing below deck on a smaller cabin cruiser. On other boats we can hear the soft quiet chatter of conversation. On one boat we hear gentle snoring.

What a strange and interesting life these floating tourists share. I can't imagine how lonely and desolate it is out on the open sea. Judging from the foreign flags hanging on some of the boats, they must have spent day's maybe weeks out alone. Strange that after traveling hours in the open waters, with just your crew, spending days on ends with no other human contact. To finally hit dry land; only to dock in this overcrowded marina, and begin living practically on top of each other. There can't be any privacy from the neighboring boats. They are tucked in tight like a can of sardines. They seem completely at ease, some are climbing onto others boats to share breakfast. An instant friendship forms with your foreign slip mates. I don't know, I think that would freak me out.

Traveling down the road towards the end of the village, we slow under a narrow stone watchtower. A final reminder of a fortress that probably once protected someone. It stands on the last dry land. The channel that surrounds it winds and turns, and then empties into the sea. Remnants of the original castle are on the corner ahead of us. Unlike Vivian's castle, the remaining part of this one is neatly kept. Every stone of the small guardhouse still in place, the rest of the castle is gone.

The man made jetties are the real architectural miracle. Long ago a plan was designed. A system installed that constricted the incoming sea. Each channel is about as wide as my neighborhood street back home. The huge stones are placed so that every hundred or so feet, a gentle turn constantly tames the incoming waves. Declan's face lights up as he proudly shows me the route. "It really is a brilliant system." He begins, "The channel is twisted, and turns at evenly spaced intervals to break the waves and control the inflow of water. The real genius at work is the vents."

He points towards a huge iron round grate on the side of one of the stonewalls. Only the top half is visible, the rest of the grate is submerged with raging water racing through the oblong holes. He begins again. "Under the village there are a number of huge stone vents, sort of like massive stone sewers. These aqueducts further tame the water and disperse the extra overage that the sea brings into the channel. The vents push the over - run of water from the channels, underneath the area where the original structure was and out the other side. Eventually leading out to the bay. The thin channels on this side of the village would have prevented the larger boats from entering the harbor. The ships that tried to invade would have to approach from the other side. The way the system was set-up they would have been sitting ducks.

The far side of the castle on the opposite side of the village was built into the hillside. This would have added even more protection. If the enemy ship tried to attack from that side of the castle they would have had the disadvantage of having water from the normal sea currents. They also would have to fight the extra push from a current they didn't know existed. The new pressure in the water that was created from the water spilling out of the submerged vents would have further exhausted the crews.

Just like the cliffs acted as a defense wall at Vivian's castle, the hilly terrain on the other side of the village would have been an added barrier. Because they would be entering the far harbor so slowly fighting the differing currents, they would have lost the element of surprise. This made them vulnerable to attack. There was a huge stonewall, and guard house on that side of the castle. The guards would have had a perfect vantage point to attack the incoming ships."

"That is quite a system indeed." I answer in awe. A memory of my dream stands vivid in my mind. The huge marauding ship waited out on the ocean. On the other side of the harbor, just waiting, as if it knew about the hidden under water currents. It wasn't going into the harbor at all. Instead it chose to wait out there. That is why Vivian knew the strong gales would shipwreck them. But why were they anchored out there? What were they doing?

I notice Declan staring at me. I quickly add, "It really is a brilliant system. I can't imagine who came up with the plan. Considering the time and the tools available. I am amazed."

Smiling he says, "I am sorry Audrey, I have run on about the architecture. What I really meant to show you was the channels themselves. We can come right through here." He points to where a path of boats enters and exits the harbor. We follow the channels when the boat traffic is quieter. We throw some food out the back of the boat and show the seal the way out of the inlet. It should be no bother at all."

I nervously look back to the harbor. "What about your Dad? He is not exactly a big fan of mine." He looks back and pauses for a moment. "My father isn't a fan of anyone, especially himself these days. Please don't take it personally." He pauses sadly before continuing, "Fair enough, he wouldn't be too jazzed about the idea of us trolling through the channel training a seal to leave the harbor, so that's why we will do it when he isn't around." I like the sound of the Captain not being around. I nod as he continues, "as luck would have it, he is leaving this afternoon up the coast to help bring some boat back. He won't be back until tomorrow in the late afternoon. That should give us enough time to get the seal out before he gets back."

I really like the plan, until he asks, "can you swim?" "Can I swim? Of course I can swim, why do you want to know if I can swim? Is there some danger in the harbor? You made it sound so easy, is there a chance we will have to swim?" I am more concerned about the frizzing of my hair. My mind races over hairstyle options.

He laughs. "Well it is always an added benefit to be able to swim whenever you are on a boat. I was wondering if after we get the seal out maybe we could head to the beach and go for a swim, I mean if you're not busy?"

My cheeks feel warm and I can sense they are flushed a bit, "Umm…great, sounds good." He smiles confidently. " Grand, I know Anna loves a day at the beach." I quickly chime in. "Great," looking down, trying to hide my disappointment. "Okay then, I would say the quietest time in the harbor is early morning. Can you meet me here before half six? That way we should have the harbor to ourselves." My voice cracks, "Did you say before 6:30 in the morning?" He nods and explains that the harbor will be the quietest around that time. The daily fishing boats will have just left.

I can't imagine waking up that early. I don't even get up that early for school. Captain McMahon's head pops up from one of the temporary piers below us. He gives a scowl when he sees Declan and whistles towards him. McMahon waves him over like he is calling his dog.

"Okay, then I will see you tomorrow." He doesn't even leave me a chance to agree to wake up that early. His back is already to me and he is heading in the direction of his father. He turns quickly back and adds. "Make sure Anna grabs her goggles, the sea water stings her." He pauses for a brief second, before adding with reassurance, "for the beach later. After we get the seal out." With that he is gone. "Yeah, for the beach later, for Anna, sounds good." I keep talking, but he is already at his father's side.

Anna, shoot: I am late to pick her up. I have to run. She will be done with activity time. I race back to the library, dodging the meandering tourists, all milling around me in slow motion without a care in the world. Doesn't anyone have anything to do today?

The last of the children stream out, Anna is behind them smiling warmly. "Did you guys come up with a plan? Declan said he thinks it will be best for tomorrow, right? I told him, I think we should go tonight," she pauses before adding in an excited whisper, "late."

We head towards the fish shop, when I realize, "Anna, we left Declan at the pub last night. When did you guys figure out this plan and why didn't you mention it earlier?" Familiar with being guarded about her answers, she waits a moment before answering. Figuring out how much information to reveal. "I wanted him to tell you the details first. Declan comes to Granny's house a lot. If Uncle Davis is umm…. having a…late night," her voice trails off, and then she adds. "Granny has a room set up for him. Aunt Mary's room."

Our last stop before leaving town is the small bridge. I take a moment to admire all the old architecture. I wonder if this beautifully arched stone bridge was built by the same person who designed the inlet system. Or was it built by whoever made the village into a fortress?

Settling on a comfortable spot on the other side of the bridge is easy with the large boulders. It is no coincidence that it is out of Captain McMahon's field of vision. I unwrap the brown paper that keeps the fish. I am surprised at how comfortable I now feel with fish membranes. I am not sure if this is something I want to share once I leave here. I throw a gross, particularly stinky head in the shallow water, and wait hoping to see if the seal is still on this side. With in a few seconds silver gray disrupts the ripples and the head vanishes.

One of the doors on a trailer at the travellers camp opens to a man I would guess to be around thirty years old. He steps out dressed in jeans and a rugby shirt. He combs back his hair and crosses the street towards town.

It is surprising how ordinary he looks. I would not even have noticed him if I had seen him around the village. I don't know what I thought a traveller would look like. Was I expecting someone dressed in colored scarves, or silky peasant shirts, maybe?

This leads me to think about Mary. Is she living in a traveller's commune? "Anna, what is Declan's mother like?" She smiles when she speaks about her aunt. "She is so nice," She smiles at the thought of her Aunt Mary. "She doesn't really say too much. She is shy and quiet. She seems kind of scared of stuff." At this observation Anna looks up at me to see if I understand what she means. I smile and nod. Anna continues her story. "She always lets me play with her makeup. My mother says she was the prettiest girl in school. The other girls were jealous of her, which is why they were so mean to her. Then when she found all the gold and jewels, the kids said she had gypsy blood in her and they accused her of stealing it. No one ever claimed any of it or came forward to say where it came from. Then she married Uncle Davis. The town people said he was after her treasure, but my Dad said it wasn't that. Dad thinks Uncle Davis truly loves her."

Anna's eyes begin to fill with tears when she mentions her father. She pulls herself together and begins again, "Dad says Uncle Davis loves Aunt Mary deeply. He just has too many issues to understand what it means to take care of a wife and son. Uncle Davis was nice at first, that's what Granny always says. She says it's the whiskey that makes him so mean. She says he must be scaring Mary somehow. He is holding something over her head." Anna wipes a stray tear before starting again. "Granny says there is no way Mary would leave and not take Declan. She is convinced he is threatening her because it would be easy enough to scare Mary. He might just be saying he would hurt Declan. But I can't imagine that, cause nobody can be that mean. Granny thinks he needs to have a conversation with the up side of her frying pan."

I sit back taking in all that Anna has said. I can't help but smile through the pain as I think about Grandma. Good old loose lips Granny. Leave it to her to spell it all out. She seems to keep a keen eye and a firm interest on her family. I would not want her angry with me in the dark, even at her age, and especially with her frying pan. She must have been a force to be reckoned with in her day.

Chapter 13

Spending the evening with Mom is turning out to be an unexpected pleasure. We are eating by the water and I find myself opening up to her in ways that I haven't been able to for a long time. I share the story of the seal, Anna's family, and the castle. I even share the legend about Vivian. Not wanting to get too carried away I leave out the part about the dreams. I haven't really come to terms with the dreams myself. I am not even sure what they are about, and there is no use in alarming my mother. That would definitely send her over the edge. How would I even start, "Oh, by the way Mom, I am pretty sure I am being visited in my dreams by the woman who may have lived in the castle. The one the locals call Crazy Lady Vivian."

Even without sharing the dreams, we are enjoying the kind of evening we haven't had in a long time, long before all the recession, lay-off crap started.

She orders a tuna tar tare, or something like that. Whatever it is called, it looks like raw pieces of chunky fish. She dips each piece in her water glass to wash the spice off before wrapping the whole thing in her napkin. Dropping the fish into her bag, she smiles and says, "Maybe we can take a walk over to see the seal later."

After dinner we stroll by the marina, admiring all the different boats. I show her the intricate channels, and the castle in the walled city. I even point out the vents. I enjoy showing off my new found knowledge of the area and I can tell she is impressed.

We stop in the open, right where Declan's father caught me in that brutal arm hold. With Captain McMahon gone, we don't have to hide. She tosses a few pieces off the dock. Within a minute a quick frenzy as a wave splashes toward us. Then the small head snaps up and grabs the tuna. She giggles with delight, "That is amazing, very good indeed."

We begin to walk towards the bridge arm in arm. Talking and laughing about old times, I point out the ever-expanding traveller's campers.

My mother stops. "Oh, I forgot to feed the seal the rest of my tuna." I point to the shallow water, "Oh, you can throw it down here, sometimes the seal comes back here. It is a lot shallower, but I think it's a place the seal comes to get away from all the traffic." She drops the last of the pieces off the bridge and they land in the water. Inside of seconds, they are taken. Each piece simultaneously, even though some have landed about a good distance from each other.

"That was strange," I say to my mother, before she has a chance to answer, I look over towards the marina. Across the inlet, on the stone road, I see Declan walking very quickly with his hands in his pockets. I am just about to yell, when a car pulls up. A girl gets out of the passenger side and a tall man with kinky hair steps out from the driver side. He protectively looks back and forth, as if he is standing guard. Declan runs towards the girl and they embrace. He holds her a long time. I strain to see her face, trying to decide if she is pretty or more importantly, prettier than me. Her back remains towards us. Both jump into the back of the car together. As quickly as it pulls up, the car speeds away. My mother and I stand speechless. I had told her about the planned boat ride, and the beach, and the disappointment over having him invite Anna.

The realization that he isn't interested in me romantically is now confirmed. I turn to Mom and in the awkward moment, I say; "look, its not like I like, liked him or anything." Always one to diffuse a sticky moment, she agrees. "Yeah, we are only here for another two weeks, and his father, total monster." I look her in the eye, "I love you Mom." She grabs me and holds me tight, "I love you too, sweetheart." As we walk over the bridge, she slips her arm through mine. "By the way, did you get a look at her shoes? Ghastly!"

I lay in bed listening to the wind howl and the storm rage as it pounds away at the skylights like a carnival strongman pounding the weight to win a prize.

It really isn't that I liked, romantically liked, Declan. I just thought he was kind of cute, that's all. I roll over to check that I set the alarm. Clicking the top allows the little green neon light to cast its dim hazy glare.

11:18 pm. I press the tiny button to catch the time. Lets face it, even if you don't romantically like a boy; it is still nice when the boy likes you. I realize the silliness to this logic and rollover again.

12:38 am. You would think he would have mentioned, I don't know in passing, just casually, that he had a girlfriend. Obviously no one has told Grandma. She would have definitely spilled it.

1:52 am. The green light seems to be five times brighter. I have to be at the back door to let Anna in, in a little more than four hours.

The dull buzz of the alarm grows louder with each second and now it screams to me. I hit it hard, really hard. I am hoping to shatter the mechanism. I throw on my favorite jeans and a dark tee shirt, pulling together the strings of my beach bag after punching a towel down. I rush to the bathroom, brush my teeth and look at my reflection. My eyes are puffy and blood shot. I begin to try to clean up some of the tiredness from my face. It is minimal damage control, at best.

Oh the heck with it. I throw my hair in braids and slap on some greasy sunscreen, before clicking off the bathroom light.

"This is the first morning we beat the Kennedys." I state proudly, grateful for the fact I don't have to watch for cow piles. The streets are quiet, no traffic. The air is incredibly clear and crisp. The rain has decided to back off leaving last night's storm to just a faint memory. Out over the countryside, the many patchwork fields of green glisten like someone shook glitter over top. I take a deep breath. A long inhale of fresh air to wake myself up.

Looking over the bridge, I begin searching for the seal. The water is quiet and calm. No movement by man or beast. The boats are quiet with only a slight swaying. A few shopkeepers begin to trickle in, but for the most part, the village is still asleep.

"We can get all the fish we want from over behind the shop. I know where my Auntie leaves it for the amateur fishermen. If we hurry we can have it. She leaves it for the taking." Crossing the road, we turn down a thin alleyway behind the library. The buildings are so close that no light can get in between. We have to move in almost complete darkness. Every time we knock into a garbage can the sound reverberates off the narrow road and the old stonewalls making an almost deafening clatter.

Anna stops in front of a set of rubber cans. I start to remove a lid, when she points to a stack of boxes. She begins removing boxes of vegetables that have been cut. The fresh parts long since removed. All that remains are the cores, seeds, and rotten or darken spots. So this is the other side of the restaurants. The smell is disgusting. Spoiling and fermenting the rotting food has been out here all night in the box, with the rain pouring over it.

She finds what she is looking for; silver dented up metal box that is an ancient cooler. Covered in bungee cords that she quickly untangles and untwists. "Why is it all tied up," I ask. She opens the box, expelling a rancid odor of decaying fish. I gag as she replies. "Cats."

We first try to find a bag or box to put the carcasses in, but everything is water soaked and falls apart at our touch. Then we try to lift the metal box in an attempt to take the whole thing. This proves far too heavy. I turn back to the rubber bin. I open the top and take out the first bag of trash. I untie the knot and dump the contents back in the bin loosely. I push the used bag around the metal box, and give Anna a nod. She pushes on her side of the metal box and the bloody fish remains fall into my used black bag. I tie it as quickly as I can. The smell of rotting fish in a used restaurant garbage bag is an odor. I can only hope I don't have to smell again, in this lifetime.

Quickly throwing the sack over my shoulder we head out the alleyway the same way we came in. Anna is the first to step out onto the street. She abruptly steps back in and pushes me into the darkness. A couple passes by engrossed in some sort of argument. Their voices soon turn into hushed tones and then fade away. I nod at Anna for her quick thinking. Who wants to explain why two girls are walking out of a dark alleyway this early in the morning carrying a bag full of butchered fish guts?

We check the road for any other people or traffic. When the coast seems clear we slink across the street carrying the seals dirty garbage dinner. Slipping down the gangway like rats, we scurry onto the piers. I can only imagine how many rodents over the last few hundred years have followed this exact path.

We have no problem finding Declan. His boat inching along in the water just in front of the dock we are standing on. He is driving the strangest looking boat I have ever seen. It is too big to be a rowboat and too small to be a fishing boat. It is sort of a combination of both. Most of the paint has either peeled or is in the process of being sanded off. It is impossible to see what color it is, or suppose to be. There isn't a cabin to speak of just an overhang. A small shelter that keeps the steering wheel and some of the instrument panels almost covered. The engine is sputtering, and gives out at regular intervals, which makes it difficult to tell whether he turned it off on purpose, or it just died. Either way, he drifts in to the slip, pushing off from the side of the pier.

"Hop on," he says. Climbing aboard, half expecting the weight of us to be enough to start it sinking. I try to hide my concern as I casually lay the awful bag of fish down at my feet. At least I won't be concerned over messing it up. Anna climbs on and sits in the ripped seat next to Declan. "You have done loads of work. She is really coming along." Anna says to Declan, who beams back at her proudly.

I take a minute to look around. Is she putting him on? She can't be serious? Did she mean this boat? I can't imagine it looking any worse. The thing is totaled. How much has he done?

After a series of failed attempts the engine finally kicks in. One last choke from the engine, a puff of black smoke and we are off. No wonder Declan waited for his father to leave town. There is no way we could discreetly travel around the harbor in this old heap.

"Now, what do we do Declan?" He looks over at me with confusion. "I guess we make sure the seal is around." I open the bag and turn my face away from the awful smell. I grab the first available piece of fish carcass and throw it into the water. The blood and entrails skim across the top and leave a bloody murky strip. Slowly bobbing on the ripples of waves moving towards the middle of the harbor.

We wait while a light rain moves in. How long should we wait?" I ask. The boat engine that has been sputtering for the entire time gives a final loud belch, and dies. Thick puffs of black smoke slip out and heads towards the sky. I watch them drift upward like a balloon that the wind yanked from a child's hand.

Declan quick to save face declares, "I think we should float out here for a while. We can throw out fish while we wait for the seal to appear." Since the engine is completely dead and we don't have any other choices we agree. Declan hands Anna an old, musty life vest.

I open the bag of fish and begin lining up the pieces largest to smallest. I grab a seat on the only section of the cushion that isn't stained or ripped. We are drifting towards a set of small fishing boats, moored in the belly of the harbor. There doesn't seem to be anyone on board, because no one comes out to protest. We are now literally leaning on the boat, almost sharing the same buoy. In fact, the only thing that keeps us from scratching and scraping the side, is the odd matched bumpers, Declan keeps throwing over. I have a feeling we are in for a long wait. I push all the fish I have so neatly lined up into the sea and throw my feet up on a deeply soiled cushion. Leaning back I am lulled by the gentle rocking of the boat, it doesn't take long to do its magic. My head on my shoulders becomes as heavy as my eyelids feel.

Chapter 14

In my dream, we are climbing higher and higher on the castles twisted steps. The lamps bob and sway with every step. Swinging the heat from the lantern, which occasionally singes my arm. The huge ruby necklace I wear bouncing on my chest as we climb. Vivian is telling me to move faster, we must get to the top. We must hurry to the castle tower.

Finally we step up the last steps, prop open the door and step into the starry night. The beautiful breeze smells of lavender. I take a huge breath. "There," she points in the moonlight. I can see the massive vessel; it bends slowly on the waves that reach high enough to grab at the sky. The night is as black as the raven's wing, making it easy to see the lights below. Lanterns everywhere, hundreds, no thousands of them light the channel below. Someone is beckoning the ships in, directing them where to go. The sea is dotted with small boats, and they are all leaving the harbor heading for the huge ship.

She is beside herself. She screams, a screech that sounds so similar to the ravens. Her screams carry so much hurt. Terrible shrills resonate from deep down inside her. She is all too familiar with the horrific scene below. The ravens that line the castle tower roof cackle and let out small protests. Vivian has a private language with these creatures. I turn to look at the pain that covers her face like a veil. Her screams fall out across the water, empty, lost in the night.

A procession of small boats moves through the channels below and towards the large ship that is anchored just outside the harbor inlet. Each overloaded with people. Some are standing straight up in the middle. Although it is far below, I can see the individuals clearly. Looking closer, many of the people look like they are tethered together. Sometimes we catch the faint echo of a cry escaping the death craft. It slowly climbs the cliff rocks before being muted by the crashing waves.

I raise my bow and draw an arrow. Vivian's hand stops me. "Save your arrows for when we can kill those tyrants. Tonight they are too far. We can't help this group. But we will free the next.

People on shore that have managed to slip away from the walled village yell and wave their arms in desperate pleas, beginning to understand the evilness of what they are witnessing. Small crude vessels occasionally launch from the beaches to try to catch the boats.

The powerful men with oars are far too strong. They wear the king's coat of arms on their uniforms. Outfits they have earned for their strength and bravery. The answer is right in front of me, yet I still ask in vain, "What are they doing? Are they helping the savages? Are they giving up their own people?" A few of the village guards begin beating at the villagers who get too close to their boats. Common village folk desperately try to free their family members are beaten and killed. All for trying to save those who are being shipped out to the pirate vessels like common cargo. Other soldiers drop their oars and begin shooting arrows, keeping the weaker people back.

Vivian slowly turns her back on the carnage below. "I am afraid we are too late. We must now search the castle and find Catherine Mary. She must have seen the boats coming. The scared girl has run off and hid again. It is good you chose to wear rubies tonight Freya. It will represent the needless blood that is shed because of greed."

Her faithful raven hops from the castle wall onto the back of her bow slung over her shoulder. His wing and the top of his head are scorched a bright orange. A battle scar, from where he was clipped by a flaming arrow that was shot by either Vivian or myself, while he dutifully protected us from intruders.

In recognition for his bravery Vivian now allows him the most favored position amongst the flock. He acts as her personal bodyguard. He is the eyes in the back of her head. When she carries her bow to hunt or battle he rides on the tip. His back almost touches her shoulder blades. Constantly and vigilantly he is watching he has her back.

The beautiful smell of the night is gone now. Replaced with an odor that travels up the cliff and enters our safe walls made of stone. It is the smell of rotting human bodies. It is the smell of suffering. The smell comes from the death ship below that loads its human bounty.

I hear the sputtering of the lanterns, a sputter, and a sputter. I open my eyes. Declan is furiously trying to start the engine, "look," he points. "Something is moving just beneath us." I follow his gaze as we float along the channels, the ones that carried the boats with the village guards that transported the human cargo.

There is movement. Something is causing a wave reaction. A fish head is bobbing; the lifeless gills are illuminated in the morning light. It seems as if part of it is missing. The engine ignites and comes alive. I grab hunks of fish pieces, heads, tails, and insides. I am throwing them as quickly as I can out the back of the boat. Declan moves the throttle and Anna pushes off from the fishing boat. We move through the channels towards the open sea.

My clothes are slightly damp from the rainy mist and I begin to feel itchy all over. My hands are pruned and smell from handling all the fish. Declan gives the go ahead, and I begin lobbing pieces over board even faster. It is hard to tell if the seal is there because the boat leaves behind a tiny wake, disrupting any seal sightings with its own pattern of waves. The engine cuts out again, and again we free float for a while. After a minute, I see a small head emerge from the dark water and grab the floating fish. Hungrily it scarfs down the food. Pointing it out to Declan sends him in another fury, to start the engine as we head outward towards the open water beyond.

Everything is proceeding as planned. The seal is following in perfect formation behind the boat. I drop a small bit of fish and he grabs hold and coasts along with us. Declan is driving the boat slow enough that the docked boats are not disturbed by the tiny wake. I grab another piece to throw to the seal when I notice he has slowed to a stop. A distance grows. His head becomes smaller as we drift away. He turns and heads back.

The engine once more quiets to a stop, this time on purpose. Declan and I look at each other. Declan says aloud what I am thinking. "Now why wouldn't he continue on out? There is nothing left back there, but a bunch of dangerous traffic that will be waking soon." He shakes his head, "Okay, we try again that's all." His voice a little deflated. He turns the boat around and we head back. I begin to prepare the fish bits. Anna's head rocks gently with the movement of the boat and I notice she has dozed off. What is it about rocking of the water; the soft swaying of the mild waves in the harbor is so soothing. Hey, it worked on me.

Smiling at the thought, I tighten the strap on her life vest, feeling relieved she is wearing one. Declan circles the boat around again and I toss a few scraps over the side. "I can't keep trolling the harbor, sooner or later the waves will wake someone, not to mention the waste of diesel." He sounds almost as tired as I feel. This time two pieces of fish go under at the same time.

"What was that?" I shout pointing to the multiple heads below. "Well I'll be, no wonder that seal doesn't want to leave, look." Declan says his excitement palpable. He points to multiple silver spots in the waters wake. There is more than one seal in here. I think you have been feeding a family." He exclaims. "I have never seen anything like that. We need to move a little slower is all, let the wee lads keep up." He pushes the gear so softly, the boat doesn't even seem like it's moving. Multiple seal heads are popping up out of the wake. I shovel fish bits overboard as quickly as I can all the while counting. There is three moving along with us. No four, no six, I can't keep track.

The seals are heading through the maze of channels. We are almost to the opening. This is so much easier than I thought it would be. I feverously begin scraping the bottom of the bag for the remaining bits of fish.

I am so engaged and excited with the seals, I don't hear the huge engine on the cruiser flying full throttle. He is barreling into the channel at top speed. He is clipping along far too fast. His yacht is aimed to hit us head on. In our haste to try to scramble out of his way we don't notice the rogue wave he is creating.

It is positioned exactly under our boat. We lift out of the water with amazing force. Even the seals are taken by surprise. The force of the wave's impact throws me against the engine. The blood from my side mixed with the last of the fish blood sticks on the rusty side panel. Staring at the concoction hides the pain for just a second. My brain puts together that I am looking at my own blood and sends an urgent message. The sting responds and begins to grow across my stomach.

I look up in time to see Anna wake. She sits in the chair next to Declan. Only the angle of the overturning boat means they are now high above me, over my head. The boat is toppling over. The sound of the boat coming down is like nails on a chalkboard, only amplified thirty times. It is a screech mixed with a whoosh. The boat seems to slow a second allowing a wall of water to descend on me.

The wave hits with such force that it slaps me hard. The entire boat springs up and over the wake that the huge vessel has just created. Anna pops up out of the depths of the green blue foam, her life preserver mimics the same spring load ejection as the boat. She pops straight up like a jack in the box. She flies past me. One minute I see her face, in seconds, I am looking at her shoes.

My body registers the trauma and amazingly goes into this self-preservation mode. I have not even pieced together what has happened. I am not quite certain where I am, when this over-whelming thought, an incredible need to swim to the surface takes over. The muscles on my arms and legs become immediately taut. They begin pushing against the waves and momentum from the boat that wants to pull me down. Strength grows inside and I kick with all my might. I too, fly towards the surface.

Anna is floating next to me, wearing almost a smile. "Are you okay?" I yell towards her. She nods, "Where is Declan?" she calls back. I look around the small boat, which is turned completely over. The wake from the huge boat is still pounding it. I can barely tread water against it. Being surrounded by the last of the fish pieces reminds me of one of those shark specials, where they throw chum over board. I glance around to see the huge boat that caused the calamity, slowly turning its massive stern. The bottom of Declan's boat begins to raise and lower against the wave in an unnatural pattern.

I can make out a form, its Declan. He is single-handedly trying to right his over-turned boat.

Swimming over to him, I ask in a winded voice, "Declan, are you okay?" His face bloody, his hair now an awful shade of reddish brown. It covers most of his features. Tangles of blood and membrane make it impossible to tell what is his blood, and what are the remaining fish parts we carried aboard. Gross pieces of carcass are strewn across the scene.

The huge boat roars to a purr, then the engine stops. A woman with a young boy climb on to the bow scurrying to come over to where we lie in the water just below. "Are you alright, is anyone hurt?" Their questions laced with worry. They are far more panicked having caused us to capsize, then we are having been capsized.

Declan whirls his head around. "Just what in the hell, would you be doing coming into the harbor at that speed. Are you mad?" A man of about sixty sticks his head overboard. "Listen, I am sorry mate, I couldn't see the channel. It came up so fast, and I couldn't negotiate her. She is new and a little bigger than I am use to. Here let me help you."

Anna is pulled aboard first, while I swim around collecting all our beach bags and miscellaneous items. Who would of thought I would be grateful for all those years of being forced to be on swim league. The capsize impact, as well as the weight of my jeans in the water, makes my legs feel like they are in concrete. Declan gives me a rough shove towards the boat, as the family grabs my arms and pull me over the side. My stomach stings with each pull.

"Come on fella, I will give you a hand." The man says to Declan. "I need to get me boat turned back around first, throw down some lines. I'll push her and you pull your boat ahead. We can yank her over." Declan says to the man in complete disgust.

Some comic relief from this ordeal comes in the form of watching Declan (just a kid) let this old rich guy have it. The man is humiliated, and keeps his head down not making eye contact, following orders completely subservient to Declan. I sit back and enjoy the show while Declan works his magic. Not only does he turn his boat right side up, he also is able to teach the man, who has nearly run us down, how to properly read the gears. Which consists of two positions forward and reverse. Declan looks back as his ugly tug, tethered to the beautiful yacht struggling to tag along.

"I am sorry Declan," is the only thing I can think to say. His boat looks about the same as it did before the accident, which still means not fit to be on the water.

"Ah, its not that bad, he has agreed to fix all the damage. I think he thinks he did more harm than he did. I guess of all the guys to blindside us out on the water, this was the best one. I mean he seems to be a rich one, right?" He takes a moment to look at the old tug before he adds, "I guess it could be a lot worse." I smile and nod back at him.

I look over the three of us. We look like drowned rats. Our clothes are soaked to the skin. We have fish particles in our hair. I pull my shirt up to see a gash across my stomach. One consolation about cutting yourself in the ocean is that the salt water cleans and disinfects the wound.

Declan's face which looked totally messed up all covered in blood, has cleaned to a small slit over his eye, and a matching one on his lip. The other blood mostly belonged to fish guts. Speaking of fish guts, Anna busies herself making little ghoulish piles of the stingy sludge.

"Did anyone see where the seals went? Are they okay?" while asking, I look in amazement at how she can without gagging, clean that fish crap up. She efficiently walks between Declan and I picking off the rank fish remnants. She places them in a neat pile on the expensive deck.

A collection of seal's circle intently around the monstrous yacht mildly dazed after the morning events. They patiently collect any stray food while keeping a close eye on us. I admire them before adding; "I can't believe they still trust us, after all that." Reaching a hand covered in fish sludge over the side, it is delicately cleaned by a small seal.

Watching the seals before responding Declan sighs, "I reckon they slipped through before the boat came in. My boat is out of commission for a while, unless we think of another plan, they may be on their own."

I sadly kick a pile of the fish bits, unaware of the extent of the frenzy below. "What do you say we head over to the beach? We can dry out in the sun. We have earned it." Declan says disapprovingly. He pauses for a moment looking sadly at his boat. "My boat is probably destroyed and we could have been killed, but what the heck?"

We all give a defeated shrug as Anna points down to the water. There in the water just below our feet, we see a very visible group of seals snatching the last bits of fish. The young are bold and the group relaxes and begins to play, gliding around in circles and flipping on to their backs.

If anything, I think we have made the situation completely unsafe for the poor guys. The entire families of seals now feel safe to frolic out in the open. They are completely comfortable to be in the midst of all the excitement of the harbor with no fear of being around all these boats. Why should they be scared, the last time they were around screaming engines, they were fed. They have even gone as far as to travel back in, probably following closely behind the huge boat and the small one it towed.

We are not just back at square one - we are worse off. We have a harbor full of trained seals. Who knows how many of these boats temporarily docked on vacation are being handled by people as capable as this guy. I glance over at the man who nearly killed us, he is sitting on a plush pillow behind the huge steering wheel, smiling meekly under his black captains cap. His wife scurries up the galley steps carrying two small glasses with a dark brown liquid lacing the bottom. She clanks the glasses as she walks. "Can I get you kids anything?" she asks.

Chapter 15

Three dejected figures slowly descend the hill that leads out of the village. At the bend, over the bridge we turn the opposite direction from the way we normally go when we are heading home.

Following another small cobblestone road, we wind around the opposite side of the marina. It also meanders around the harbor, before it turns then heads up past the old rectory.

They must have rebuilt the church after the fire that the librarian had mentioned. It's funny, it doesn't look new, but I guess around here "new" is a subjective term. The exterior is stone so maybe most of the damage happened inside, since the outside still looks really old.

The honorable stone gravestone crosses are gorgeous. Intricate Celtic patterns, with stone carvings raised in beautiful braided designs throughout. Each Celtic form is so unique yet; they all have similar outlines consisting of the large circle with the thick cross inside.

Gravestone's sprout out of tufts of grass. Clusters speckle the side yard of the rectory. Each one proudly and majestically looks out to sea.

I have never seen the village and the harbor from this perspective. The view is equally magnificent, as all the others. The mountains surround the backside of the village. The intricate channels weave their way through. The castle watchtower stands visible on the very edge of land.

"That's it!" I yell. Both Declan and Anna raise their crestfallen heads. Exhausted and defeated, but still mildly curious, they wait to hear my thought. "The vents, we could use the vents. Declan, didn't you say they travel under the village and let out on the other side of the marina, to a larger basin?"

His entire demeanor perks up, as he nods in agreement. "We could take the seals through there and then let them out the other side. That way, they wouldn't have to travel through the busy channel and they would be free of the harbor traffic. We wouldn't be dropping them into the major ocean, either. They could get use to the rougher waves and the little guys could learn to maneuver their way around. Free of those crazy tourists."

"Brilliant, Audrey." Declan begins. "It is quite a bit trickier than through the harbor, and will take an incredible amount of planning. It's a maze under there. Twisting tunnels, it is a vast intricate system. We would have to make sure we plan the best route. I have been down there many times before, so I know the system. I have actually made a few drawings. We would have to pry the grates off the front but wait, I know one that is beginning to give, and I can get in it easy enough."

Anna and I can see the wheels in Declan's head turning and we all start to feel the excitement. He wrings his hands before saying. "We will need to make sure the tide is low so there is plenty of air space. But it could work, it definitely could work."

I can tell he is impressed with my idea. Who am I kidding? I am impressed with my plan too. Our pace picks up, as we all add ideas on how we can make the ancient sewers under the city work. I am equally fascinated with Declan. That was some pretty quick thinking and reflexes out on the water today. He also has a keen sense of the history, and he has even drawn out some plans of the aqueducts. We are almost at a trot heading over the last hill, leading to the beach.

We cut through a small path that is over grown with prickly bushes and weeds. I immediately recognize the nettles and keep my hands close to my body to prevent a sting. The path drops off to a muddy patch of sand, and then unfolds to a splendid stretch of beach. The tide is low, allowing a huge space to picnic. Some families have already laid claim to spots and are busy unfolding blankets.

Down the beach, we see a solitary figure sitting on a blanket. "Look, it's Mom." I feel a great sense of relief to see her. That was a rough morning. I truly feel as if I need her right now.

She eyes us up and down. A look of concern covers her face. "Are you okay?" Anna begins to fill her in on the details, when I quickly interrupt, "is that lunch? I am starved." I shoot Anna a glare to tell her to nip it. The last thing we need is my mother putting a stop to the whole operation. In America, at least in Charlotte where I am from, kids aren't allowed to go risking their lives. Capsizing in boats and swimming through ancient glorified sewers, isn't really something my parents are going to give the go ahead on.

"Yes, that is lunch, I made some sandwiches and brought snacks. Deidre and your father are going to try to finish up early and join us for a cook out later. Why don't you guys go wash up either in the bathroom or ocean, and then you can dig in." My mother says, turning her head slightly sideways. I can read her eyes and they are filled with an abundance of questions. I can tell I am going to have some explaining to do, but it can wait until later.

We all opt to clean off in the ocean, and hurry down to the sea. It is a beautiful blue green, with the small outcroppings of rocks. "We need to be careful, no talk about going into the sewers in front of my mom otherwise she will blow a gasket, agreed." Anna and Declan nod. After a quick soak back in the cold water, we head up and devour my Mom's picnic. Capsizing in a failed attempt to free a family of seals does in fact leave one famished.

Declan invites me to view his architectural renderings of the village, being careful not to mention the underground vents or sewers in front of my mother. We agree that I will head back with Declan and Anna tonight. He proudly explains how he has taken an evening adult course to learn how to draw architectural plans to scale. I feel relieved that he will have a fairly accurate depiction of the waterways below.

The rest of the day is spent swimming and playing on the beach. In the water, Anna and I mimic some of the antics we have seen the seals do. It is so wonderful to let loose and enjoy our selves. The water is so cold, and many of the locals wear wet suits.

The Irish beach is so different then the beaches back home. There are no lifeguards, and no signs to warn of underwater rip tides. Even though everyone knows they exist and is careful. In recent years, this area has become something of a small surfing community. So many of the teens start dotting the beach with boards tucked under their arms. There are no bronzed or muscle beach bums. The air is far too chilly, and the water is freezing for skimpy suits. Some people are foolish enough not to apply sunscreen, and their fair skin is already beginning to pink.

At the beach back home, you spend the day lying on the towel sweating. Then you run in the cool ocean, then back to the towel, where you almost immediately start sweating again.

Here there is always a cool breeze blowing, so you are never really that hot. Then when you do go in the ocean, the water is so cold you can't stay in that long. You rush back to your blanket, and wrap a towel around yourself to keep warm.

My father and Deidre arrive with still more supplies. Declan and Dad spend a great deal of time and effort on a small tin tray with a layer of coals at the bottom. They take turns, one tries lighting, one tries to block the wind. After much ado the small tin tray finally smokes and the flame ignites the coal bricks. Carefully, they lay the grate over top and start cooking sausages. The warmth of the makeshift grill and the smell of the sausages grips and holds everyone close. Deidre and Mom lay out even more platters of coleslaw and casseroles. Considering how rocky the morning started, the afternoon has turned wonderful, and the evening is beginning to be nicer still. I am anxious to see the drawings and plan out a strategy to safely get the seals out of the harbor.

A young man a little older than Declan wanders over towards our blankets. He is tracking and kicking sand on us with his heavy boots. He isn't dressed for an evening at the beach; he is wearing jeans and a sweatshirt that are soiled and sooty. He looks like he is wearing the same uniform I have seen Declan and his father wear after a day at the marina.

"Evening folks, Declan, I have a message from your father. The water level is too low; he can't get the boat down the coast without heading out to deeper waters. He wants to wait it out a day or two. He will wait for the water to rise before he starts back. He will leave at the first sign that the tide is rising."

I am so glad to hear the news. This means one; the water level is low, so we shouldn't have any problems moving through the tunnels. Two; we won't have to worry about running into Declan's father.

Declan also seems noticeably happy about the news. "No bother, thanks. Listen John did you bring your mobile?" The stranger begins feeling around in his pockets before answering. "Yeah mate, it's in the car. You need to use it?" Declan sits up and brushes some sand off. "Yeah can I?" John is quick to answer, "No problem, I will take you it is just over the hill." Declan seems a little nervous at the idea of the guy joining him to make his call. "No bother, I can find your car. Toss me the keys and then you have a sausage."

The man looks like he is about to decline. My mother and Deidre move in for the kill. Deidre insists while my mother's starts piling a plate for the guy. I watch Declan as he walks briskly towards the knoll. After a few paces he breaks into a run. He is out of sight within a matter of seconds.

It is obvious by his actions; he wants to use the phone alone. I am sure it has something to do with our plan to release the seals. He returns after a few minutes. This time, he doesn't even sit down, "I umm, need to go. Uhh, something has come up with Uncle Ted. He needs me to help move the cows." Deidre looks up, "Didn't you move the cows out of that pasture last night?" He searches the ground, "umm

141

yeah, but we missed some." My mother and I look to each other. We know for a fact he didn't move cows last night. We saw him down at the harbor, with that girl. Declan is a horrible liar.

Wait a minute, I look at Deidre, don't tell me she is buying this load? Surely she can tell he is lying? Does anyone else notice what a crappy liar Declan is? People, please.

He says a quick thank you, trying not to look towards Anna or me. He shrugs his shoulders and softly digs the sand with one foot and then drops it onto his other foot. John looks up with a chunk of sausage in his mouth. "You need a lift? Just give me a sec..."Declan cuts him off before he can finish. "No listen, I got it, Uncle Ted is in town, I can go get a lift off him..." His voice trails off. He is such a crappy liar. I can tell with every word he says he is full of it. I can't believe anyone is buying this. He turns on his heel and heads out.

I jump to my feet, there is no way I am going to let him just leave and just slime out of his obligation. I chase after him and wait till I am out of earshot of my parents. "What about our plan, Declan?" He stops in his tracks, without turning around, his back still to me he gives a curt answer. "Oh yeah, can we do it maybe tomorrow?" I am trying to hide my disappointment and anger. I wait a second to catch my breath. "Tomorrow? You heard that guy. Your father could be heading back, besides what about the tide, and the seals? You see how comfortable they are around the boats. You know how dangerous it is for them now. We need to do this, every minute counts. What is up?"

I can tell he knows. I know there is more to this. He turns back and looks me straight in the eye. "Audrey, I am sorry, but I have to do this. I can't worry about some family of seals right now. Anna can show you the

142

plans." He stops and puts his head down. Another obvious tell, that he is about to lie again. "I will come by later to Grandmas. I can go over them then, okay?"

I see the headlights illuminate the side of the sandy bluff. Someone has come to pick him up. I am now more convinced then ever he is meeting that girl again. He is blowing us all off, he is putting those poor seals in jeopardy, just to hang out with his girlfriend. I can't believe this.

Turning away from him, so he won't see my hurt and disappointment. I take a deep breath. Pushing away the tears that are filling my eyes. "What- ever. See ya." I turn back composing myself, it is no use. Declan is gone.

I brush it off, just like the rest of the dirt and coarse sand that is stuck all over me. I walk back towards the glow of the coals on the tiny grill. I sit down across from my mother and look her right in the eye. She knows how I am feeling.

She stands, "come on Audrey, help me find somewhere to throw out this trash." With that, we walk into the darkness. We aren't carrying any trash, but everyone on the blanket is so engrossed in their festive evening, they don't even notice.

"I can't believe it, he lied. We know he was in town last night." I begin just unloading on my Mom. "I know Audrey, I knew he was lying too, but what can we do? It's not our business. Whatever that young man is up to, it has nothing to do with us. He is playing a dangerous game with all those lies, and running around with, well who knows?" She shakes her head. His obvious deception has put her off.

After we walk for a while, the anger and disappointment settle and disperse. My mother senses it and speaks up, "the only people that young man has to answer to is his parents. If they don't seem to care where, or what he is up to, I am not sure if we have a right to, either. It's not like he wants our help. Whatever he is doing, he wants to be doing it. It's a shame, really." She shakes her head before continuing. "I don't even feel comfortable saying anything to Deidre, especially tonight, she seems so happy."

My mom is right, he does seem to be making his own decisions, and both of his parents have kind of abandoned him. Besides Deidre does looks happier tonight then I have ever seen her before. What do we really know about this guy? Look at his father; maybe the apple doesn't fall far from the tree, after all?

Declan doesn't owe the seals or me anything. It is his choice. I am going ahead with the plan without him. He gave me permission to look over his drawings. I will check them out with Anna. It has been Anna and me from the start. I don't have long staying here in Ireland and I am going to enjoy it.

We head back to the picnic. I grab a seat next to Anna and put my arm around her. "Just cause Declan isn't here, doesn't mean you and I can't hang out. How about we go over the drawings ourselves? We can see if we can make heads or tails of them." Anna's face lights up. "Mom can Audrey sleep over tonight, please?" Deidre looks over at me her eyes brighter than I ever seen them before. "Sure, if it's okay with Audrey and her parents." My mother searches my face before giving a nod.

If I thought Anna's house was cool last time I was here, I am even more impressed now. The upstairs is vast with huge rooms and multiple levels, connected with varying size staircases. The main hallway is wide with doors on every side, each holding a bedroom. The rooms are immense, each with their own fireplace and bathroom. We stop at one near the end of the hallway. "We can put your stuff in my room." Anna proudly shows off her temporary room. It is the size of my parent's room at home, with two huge windows. The corner is littered with boxes, some open with toys spilling out. It looks as if Anna moved in quickly. The room is decorated in reds and browns and aside from the toys; you would never know this is a kid's room. There is a massive bed in the middle of the room, with a dark wooden canopy.

Dropping my overnight bag near her bed leaves me ready to explore this cavernous house. Anna leads me down the opposite end of the hallway to another hidden staircase. This one leads to another floor, with another set of doors. This hallway is quite a bit narrower than the first one. Most of the bedroom doors are closed. The few that are open, show rooms that are smaller than those on the floor below, but still there is a stately grandeur about them. All the ones I see have their own fireplaces, just like the ones on the floor below.

The end of the hall opens to a library of sorts, with shelves run floor to ceiling. Each one piled high with books. A few of the volumes look ancient. Most are stacked randomly, and mix - matched. Some back to front, some upside down. It is hard to believe anyone can make heads or tails of what is here.

A large desk stands in the center of the room, littered with drawing plans. A few are rolled, but most are lying flat or in the process of being flattened with books holding down the corners.

"Are these all Declan's?" I ask. Anna steps beside me leaning over my bent shoulder. "Yeah, I think so. There are lots of etchings around here because my Aunt Mary draws as well." She further unrolls a set before agreeing, "yes, these are Declan's."

Proudly she presents me a small hand made portfolio. It is made of dark cardboard stock and held together by a large piece of velvet green ribbon that has been neatly pulled into a bow.

Once untied she carefully opens the flap, letting a faint odor of age escape with a few of the etchings. Picking up one from the floor, I notice that these are done in a much more delicate style. The work of an uncertain artist, many of the lines are barely there, broken and scratchy. Two separate, but both talented artists at work. Declan's work is far more technical and confident, like a draftsman.

"These are my Aunt Mary's." Anna adds boastfully. Mary's are more like a fine artist's renderings. I pull another in for closer inspection. It is a pencil rendering of a castle. It takes only a moment for my brain to process and register what I am looking at. It is Lady Vivian's castle. The one I have seen in tact only one other place in my dreams.

This can't be a coincidence. How does Mary know what the castle looks like? Has she seen it in a book perhaps? I look up at the colossal collection on the shelves. Perusing the covers, I try to find one on castles. Many don't have titles. Even their spines are blank. It will take hours to look through them all. Discouraged I grab Mary's portfolio and put it down on the other side of the desk. An attempt to put it far from where I will be working, some needed distance, if only in my head anyway. I am not ready to think about Vivian or the castle, or how it could be connected to Mary. Not now, anyway. I have a family of seals that I need to help first. I will look through her work. After I examine the plans.

Declan has made incredibly detailed drawings of the sewers and aqueducts under the village. Every part of the road, the channels and the castle that once stood at the edge of what was part of the walled village, has been accounted for. He has carefully drawn and measured each space. He has views from every angle. I pull back page upon page, admiring his precision. I neatly roll them back, until I find what I am looking for. "Anna look I think I found it."

It is plans for a set of tunnels or sewers. "Is this under where the castle was?" I look towards Anna. These are so confusing. I wish Declan could help us. I can barely make sense of these intricate drawings. Anna steps over and takes a long look at the plans. "I am not sure. Yes look there, that is the vent that faces out to the harbor at the curve in the road near the library." I follow her finger, and slightly turn my head, trying to figure out where she is. "Yes, Anna. Thank you. I see, now it's starting to make sense." Look, he has even shown where the grates are on top of the ceiling of the tunnels. Right here, this one is on the road in front of the library." I nod as I silently thank Declan for a job well done.

Based on his drawings, there seems to be a main chamber that takes most of the over flow water from the channels. This directs the water through almost a straight line of tunnel that travels under the width of the village. There is a huge grate on the opposite side that pushes the water out into the hillside and down to the larger basin that leads to the sea. Off the main aqueduct, there appears to be many smaller ventricles that twist and turn under the rest of the village. Here is where the old sewers hook up to the present day system. The modern day one is connected at different intervals. Allowing access to present day manholes. Some have small ladders attached. If I travel down the wrong tunnel and the tide should fill, I could climb out there. The only problem is, I won't be able to lift the huge cement cover. Not to mention what to do if the seals are following? I can't exactly ask for them to climb the staircase and climb out to the road above. It is still nice to know they are there if I need them.

The first problem I see, based on the precise drawings Declan has made, is getting into the system in the first place. I may be able to squeeze through the wiring that forms the grates, but I don't think I will be able to coax the seals to follow. Declan mentioned one is loose, but I will need to check on the other side of the village at the outlet grate. I need to see the grate that leads to the larger basin and then the open sea. The problem is how.

The vent lets out on the hillside into the water. Based on Declan's plans, each of the larger vents that open to the sea come equipped with a toggle to release the metal grate. I am not sure if that has been added as a modern convenience, or whether that is part of the initial design. If it is part of the original design, there is no way it would still be working. I would have to be able to repel down the side of the hillside in order to see if it is operational, or if it is loose enough to pry open. "Anna do you have paper and a pencil?" She grabs some and hands it to me. She grabs a book from the overloaded shelves, curls up on an overstuffed chair and begins reading. I write down on the paper in bold letters: Exit Grate.

I find a grate sort of close to the exit, but it is on the road. So far, that is the closest one that would let the seals into the larger basin. I guess the best thing to do is to go down tomorrow and get inside. How will I remove the heavy grate? How will I get in? Even with Declan, it will be tricky. The next thing I write down is: Tools.

From Declan's intricate plans, I am able to draw smaller maps of the route, ones that I will be able to understand and take with me. I have a route I feel will be the straightest and easiest to free the seals. I include where the present day storm drains and sewers connect to the ancient system, as well as any manholes.

Raising my head to stretch my neck, I see Anna has fallen asleep in the chair. Standing and stretching makes me realize how long I have been at it. I pull a throw over her and head back to the desk. Browsing the bookshelves, I see one book about the moon. I grab it and quickly check the index in the back for tides. I flip to the chapter. Tides come in and out in twelve-hour increments. I write Tides on my list.

Feeling confident with what I have done, I pick up the makeshift portfolio of Mary's and sit in the comfortable chair across from Anna. Another drawing escapes out as I open the portfolio.

Slowly it floats to the floor. I have to make a conscious effort to focus my tired eyes. The drawing lands with the image side up.

I am so familiar with the beautiful face that stares back from the sketch. Even without the gaudy, over the top jewels or a raven perched on a bow. I would recognize Vivian anywhere.

My tired eyes perk awake. Slowly, with shaking hands, I lift the portrait. There is no way someone would be that familiar with the subject of their portrait unless they had spent time with the model. Could Mary have had the same dreams as I? Many are of the castle from inside when it was intact. I sit straight up in the chair, how can this be? Rushes of cold chills run through my veins cooling my blood.

The grand hall with the heads from the various hunts mounted on the walls. The kitchen with the massive hearth and the herbs hung to dry. On one page alone she has multiple sketches and angles, all depicting the castle, or Lady Vivian, or the grounds around the castle. Mary spent far more time at this mystical place in her dreams than I have. She must have returned over and over. There are some places in her drawings I haven't seen. There are bedrooms, a cellar of some kind, hallways and guardhouses. Her attention to detail is amazing. Every nuance of the castle or Vivian's face has been captured on paper with her delicate pencil strokes.

Some of Mary's drawings are drawn with a heavy hand. The pencil strokes dark, and the shadows are darkened by pencil lead being applied over and over again. Smudged and labored, over-worked and dark as if they have been done by someone haunted. I sense her sadness. It is so obvious to me the line between her dreams and reality have blurred. One drawing in particular sends a shiver of fear over me. It is a picture of a man who holds a torch, while strapped to his back, a large sword. The lines are dark and smudged, the drawing is over worked, but I can still make out his expression. His face contorted in pain and anger, his mouth open. He appears to be screaming or shouting. Seeing this scene turns my cool blood to ice.

Exhaustion finally takes over. I fall back asleep on the comfy chair. The drawings drop from my lap, onto the floor. I fall deeper and deeper into the cushion, as they sway back and forth with the tide.

Chapter 16

The boat we travel on is far too small for the turbulent waters. The ocean spray slaps me, as a freezing rain pounds down on us. With each wave comes a fresh assault of a salty sting on my face and eyes. I grab the oars and row with all my might. My stomach muscles pull and tear with each stroke. The tip of the boat climbs high above my head. The immense ocean waves, once again, ready to overpower us with every swell. The violent sea stands angry tonight. How dare we disturb her magnificent whitecaps with our crude boat? She reminds us once more that it is the ocean that holds the ultimate power, and we must admire her surges, and admit that it is the sea's energy that reigns supreme. Vivian looks up at the heavens and screams at the top of her lungs, "Oh great sea, you are the mighty beast, please let us pass. For we want only to go home with our small spoils."

Grateful, she has acknowledged the keeper of the breakers. There is a far more clear and present danger against us tonight. We are being chased. There is a larger craft gaining on us. Manned by many oarsmen. They will soon overpower us. We must paddle faster. I am using all my might. Separating Vivian and I on the boat lay bodies, crumpled, and broken. Sacks of sugar and tea mixed with a bag of silver lay between them. We grabbed whatever we could, before they detected us aboard their ship that travels here from the Far East.

Continually, we are shaken and thrown with each wave in every direction. We are battered. The cliff wall is illuminated by moonlight. I hear my voice scream out, "we won't make it through tonight. We have missed the opening."

We will be crushed against the side. We are going to break into splinters, smash to smithereens. Vivian expertly turns the oar and places it straight down. Acting like a rudder, it sends the boat into a razor sharp turn. The boat behind us is not as fortunate. It smashes against the rocks. The smashing sound of the impact is followed by the sound of wood and bone splintering.

We scrape against the rock as we look for the cave opening. Thanks to Vivian's steering, we now are parallel to the cliffs. The boat flinches and slows again. It floats on a massive wave, before it is thrown toward what appears to be a dark fissure on the side of a boulder. The wood on the sides of our craft shaves and whittles from such an abrupt approach. The friction gives off heat. We barely squeeze through a crevice; a cave opening that is in the shape of a dagger.

Suddenly we are out of the bitter elements. Transported out of the violent waters and into a silent dark cave. The once turbulent water now becomes a quiet meandering lake. Our boat gives a shiver, then rocks one last violent shake, copying the last of the fierce waves outside, and then it gently follows the pattern of the water.

I catch my breath. A realization passes over me. I have danced with death again. "I thought we would die, several times this evening." My words echo off the inside of the cave. I am answered with complete silence, total darkness.

The ravens returning from battle interrupt the quiet whisper of our oars slowly gliding rhythmically through the water. They fly in formation towards the inner recesses of the cave. Some are returning from the slave ship, while others were waiting to make sure no oarsman survived the crash on the rocky cliffs outside. Either way, they fought alongside us bravely and valiantly. It was the many diversions that allowed us to board the vessel and take so much cargo.

I can't even see my hand before my face. It is black as coal. Vivian slowly, expertly glides the boat through the snake like channel. Occasionally, a raven flies to close and I can feel the tickle from their feathers.

In the distance, a faint glow. The light grows brighter. We float towards it. Entering our small basin, the hidden marina feels safe and dry. The cave walls are sheer and when I look up it looks as if the cliff has been hollowed out inside. All of the walls have torches placed in holders. Catherine Mary has prepared for our return. Too afraid to help with the fight, she has been keen enough to keep the home fires burning.

Vivian stops the boat under a huge standing wrought iron candelabrum that holds at least twenty candles. We quickly pull the boat up to a small wooden pier. Vivian lifts a huge cloth bag, coins, and metal clank against each other. Crumpled in a corner of our boat lie the people, tattered and broken. Clothes, torn, skin raw and ripped in spots. Bruises in purple, blue and neon green freckle their faces.

I grab a skeleton like body. So cold to the touch - I repel back from their smell, a mix of sweat, blood, and fear. One man's shirt is torn away and he exposes multiple cuts and contusions. He can barely raise his head. Vivian places a limp arm over her shoulder.

She prepares to climb the stairs, she stops and looks back, "leave the sacks at the door and then help the people." I stumble a little over the weight of the loot we got tonight. I hear clanking of metal inside. She looks at me, her voice spiked with a tone of guilt. "I took what we needed, I help the people first." Her eyes have that far away look. Looking closely, I see terror, confusion, and death staring back at me. We line them up in front of the fire, trying to keep them warm. They barely stand undernourished, beaten, and terrified. Many speak with a foreign tongue.

We have heard the stories before, yet some feel the need to share it. Their voices falter, some have accents, some inaudible. One thing for certain, each speaks of the same terrifying story.

It is one that always starts with the ships. The boats travel the coastline of many different lands; out to sea for months.

Buying people, stealing people, whatever means it takes to fill the ships. Shackling them together on the ships before moving on. Squeezing them in tight to make room. These ships have come for cargo. Dry goods or human goods. These ships will be filled before the long trip back.

Vivian paces behind our half dead guests. The events of this horrible evening are beginning to trigger the demons in her head. The pacing becomes more animated and her agitation grows more apparent. Spooning the warm broth into hungry mouths, I keep one eye on Vivian. The people gathered are dazed and mute. Some begin to look towards Vivian. There is fear in their eyes.

They have faced unspeakable evil tonight and survived. Now as they sit in front of the kitchen hearth, frozen and dying, they are dealt another terrifying blow. Fear grows from the realization they are staring madness in the face. The shivers that radiate off there bodies are a reaction to Vivian. She begins her ranting, rocking and sobbing. She quietly chants and mutters. Her eyes fill with so much pain. Horrible cries of pain and torture. She is slipping into one of her flashbacks. I want to scream at them all, you don't know her. She is a beautiful flower. Stop judging her. Instead I look away beaten down by exhaustion and embarrassment. In the background she screams her raven shrill scream.

"CAAAHHHHHH." I open my eyes awakened by the raven just outside the window. I am back in the library. Anna is in the chair across from me sleeping peacefully.

Watching the sun begin to rise out over the countryside, I look at the drawings scattered around me on the chair and at my feet. Mary, Declan's mother, is part of Vivian's story. We both walk in that surreal world.

Is the treasure Mary found Vivian's? Are these dreams real? These dreams are they snippets of time misplaced in our brains? What about poor Vivian? She is riddled with guilt, sorrow and insanity. But why does she come to me? Why am I in this? What purpose do I serve? Who is going to listen to some random kid from the states? I wonder if Declan knows about his mother and Vivian.

Speaking of Declan, where is he? He never even came back last night. He was going to check on our plan. I haven't forgotten about the seals. I need to solve this problem in this time first. Before I go looking for more ghosts in the past. I smile to myself at the thought of looking for ghosts. I am not looking for anyone. Instead, the past has been hunting me since I got here, and if I am not careful it is going to catch up with me sooner rather than later.

Chapter 17

The walk to the village this morning is quiet. More than quiet. I would say it is down right somber. After dropping Anna for reading group, I head over to the underground tunnels.

There is an old broom on the dock that I borrow. Using the handle I take a few swipes at the toggle, and after a couple of jabs the vent opens easily. This will give enough access for us to pass through. I follow the tunnel above ground, my crude sketch in tow. The route is straight forward enough. Having accounted for each vent, I check them off making note of every vent that is above. On the other side of the village, exactly where Declan's drawing indicated, is our exit vent. It lays midway on a hill, below it the toggle. After that a sheer drop to the ocean below. It will be impossible to scale down and check the lever. I collect about twenty rocks of varying sizes and begin throwing them towards the toggle, most fall short. Some land directly on.

Either way, there is no way to see if the lever is operational. A sudden whoosh sound releases a huge wave of blue green sludgy water. It batters against the vent, leaving a pile of debris stuck to the metal grates before the water spills down the ravine and into the sea below.

When I make it to this point inside the vents with the seals, I will have to have already released the grate, or the seals and I will be thrown into the side with the same force as that debris just was.

Wait a minute, how does that crap get cleaned out of the vent? I mean wouldn't there be a constant build up there? Yet when I first got here, it was clean. I look around hopeful that there must be a way to get in. Someone is keeping the drain clear.

Looking around the hillside, I spot a tiny path that cuts back on the other side. I scamper up the hill and climb down easily, finding the trail that meanders under an outcropping. My heart beats faster as I pull back some tall weeds.

I find a clearing that opens to a door. Not really a door, it is more of an opening that has been covered with a wide piece of wood, still, I am relieved to see it. To me it is a gift, because it represents a way out. A little more brushing off and I find a standard door handle and lock. With a few thrusts and kicks, I am able to open the homemade contraption. The bottom scraps across the cement below, sending out a sound like nails on a chalkboard.

I step inside to the sudden rush of cool air. It is dark, dank and all together creepy. An odor of musty gross sewer greets me. I bob and weave to avoid the cobwebs. Down the long storm tunnel, there is a thin layer of watery bilge, with roots seaweed and the occasional litter of trash. It appears as if it will be up to around my shin. I hadn't weighed the "gross" factor of this particular endeavor, but now seeing the disgusting water, I realize I will be walking through a sewer. My body involuntarily convulses into a shiver.

Glancing up to see the ceiling I make a note to self; wear a hat. Judging from the look of the filth and the size of the cobwebs it is safe to say I will be showering for a week straight. The concrete sidewalk I am on thins quickly, and disappears into a cement molding that drops off into the sludge. I only have around five feet before I am unable to walk this way.

I will have to be able to lure the seals up from the drain and onto the concrete path, if I am to bring them through this way. I look down the dark tunnel, and debate whether I should continue walking the tunnel. It gets super dark, and I decide I will need more tools, specifically a flashlight, before I head in further.

I climb back on the cement sidewalk. Before leaving through the door I lean over the metal banister that has been installed and reach for the vent. The other side of the toggle is almost in my grasp. I lean a little further, when the burning pain in my stomach stops me. I lift my shirt and look at the cut I received yesterday, when the boat capsized. It is healing slowly, but still raw and sore, a red irritated ring has formed around it.

I will have to be careful not to aggravate it during the journey. I climb back out into the sunshine and find a seat on the top of the hillside. Pulling out my notes, I begin a list of supplies. I write the word hat, and then underline it. The list grows quickly, and upon closer inspection I realize I don't have near enough money to buy all this stuff, even with all the oversized coins my mom gives me for groceries. I will need to borrow as much as I can.

Stepping onto the metal pier, I see Declan is bent over helping push a boat off. He throws the lines to a young boy who is onboard. "Hi, glad to see you back." Is about the only clever thing I can think to say.

He looks up, "Audrey, I was going to come looking for you. I am sorry about last night." He looks as if he is going to elaborate. I have important business to deal with so I skip the story and jump to the point.

"Your drawings are really amazing, thanks for letting me look through them. I was able to follow them. I need to ask another favor. Would you be able to lend me some stuff?" His face looks relieved, he also has no interest in rehashing last night. "Of course, listen I still want to help. It is pretty quiet here." He looks down at my list and sketch of the tunnels before asking, "Can we go over it now?"

We pick up Anna, grab a few croissants and make ourselves comfortable. I explain the route and some of my observations having just walked it from above ground. "Brilliant, you got it really well planned." There is an audible impressed tone in his voice. If the truth were known, I am proud of myself. My plan will work regardless of who goes with me.

Declan's voice breaks my thought, "My father is coming back tomorrow, so I think we need to do this tonight, not too late. The tunnels will be dark enough as it is, so we should try to use as much of the evening light as we can. With the last of the sun, and a couple of flashlights that should give us all the light we need."

We all agree and head over to the boathouse to scrounge up the tools we think we will need. We grab only what we can stuff into a moldy old duffel bag. We agree to leave this stuff in the vent. Declan climbs down a small cloth ladder he has rolled up, and moves the toggle on the huge vent. The old metal reluctantly sways and opens halfway. He drops into the tunnel and turns extending his arms. I toss him the old duffel and drop down. I swing my body and the momentum from my thrust sprays Declan with water. I land on my hands and knees in the water lining the base of the sewer. The good news is the sludge is mostly seawater being the entrance, so it's relatively clean. Still there is a stench given off, and I quickly jump to my feet. We stash the bag on a small ledge towards the top of the tunnel. Declan gives it a hard push to make sure it will stay.

Anna spends the rest of the late morning tying rope to the grates all along the route. Once she is comfortable with the knot, she drops them down inside. These will act as guides, as well as extra handles, if we need to steady ourselves along the route. Some of the grates are in the middle of busy roads. At times, we have to get creative in order to gain access to the vents while traffic tries to skirt around us. Anna stands in front of me and pretends to be upset about her missing cat. Cars lay on their horns. Sometimes they barely miss us, nearly colliding with the other lane of traffic as they over correct to avoid us.

On the super busy sections I tie the rope check the knot, and drop it down between the grates as quickly and efficiently as I can. There is no time to check if I have tied it tight enough. It is a wonder someone hasn't called the Gardaí, or worse yet our parents, to report our strange behavior.

We run back to the fish shop. Anna's Aunt helps a customer while we try to wait patiently. It seems like a prison sentence. She can't decide what to serve her guests for dinner. I nervously tap the last of the mud and sludge from my boots, "Girls, where is the fire? What can I do you for?" Aunt Carol seems amused at our obvious impatience. Anna goes into a long elaborate description of the seals and the busy traffic in the harbor, and our plan to help them out. In fact, she goes into such great detail, I am afraid she is going to mention the tunnels, and I am just about to kick her on this side of the counter, when Carol asks, "You wouldn't be thinking of some daft idea, like going down in those tunnels, would you lassie?" Without missing a breath, Anna looks her aunt straight in the eye, and says, "Of course not, there is no way I am going down in those tunnels." Her Aunt smiles confidently. "Good girl darling, there are all kinds of dangers down there. That's no place for a young lady to be," that said she begins packing up fish parts. She turns to grab another roll of brown paper.

Anna smiles and winks at me. We both know she didn't lie, but she didn't really tell the truth about the tunnels either. Anna whispers. "She didn't ask, if you were going in those tunnels." I smile back, one of my fake smiles. Having heard the warning, and the smell of all the dead fish has turned my stomach sour. We leave the shop with a large bounty of seal food, and a promise that all the rest of the bits and pieces from the day will be left at the rear of the shop for us for tonight.

We dart back to the pier and begin throwing bits over to attract the seals. They are starving today, and it takes no time for us to lure them over to the vents. We drop the rest of the fish at the opening. Taking turns throwing pieces through the holes in the grate.

The younger, smaller seals are able to easily swim through some of the vents that are bent. The larger ones eat the pieces outside the grates. They seem as comfortable in the tunnels as they do outside in the marina.

Making a game out of darting in and out, we have no problem leaving them frolicking in their new spot. They seem to enjoy the quiet of being in this small area that boats can't fit into. The whole atmosphere seems to relax them more.

I stop to see that Declan is clear on the plan for later. I want to be sure he hasn't double booked with his girlfriend again tonight. He assures us he is ready and anxious to move the seals out. As we cross the bridge, I notice how busy the harbor is. In fact, it is busier than I have ever seen it before. It's a good thing we are moving them out tonight. If we wait any longer, there is sure to be some sort of accident.

We have a few hours to grab some rest before heading back into town. Lying down in bed I realize I am far too excited to sleep. My mind replays the plan over and over again, trying to anticipate any problems. I don't want any surprises down there. Sleep comes after all the events of the past few days are finished catching up. I awake to the alarm ringing, a restful couple hours makes me feel stronger and more confident than ever. A flicker of sadness passes when I recall that my sleep was dreamless. I find comfort in knowing that Vivian travels with me. Her courage and prowess that serves in so many challenges before protects me like a cloak.

Anna trots over the field, covering the huge pasture in what seems like a split second. She is at the back door wearing a goofy smile. Grabbing a baseball cap, I pull my hair into a ponytail and wind it through the small hole in the back. My mother watches with mild interest. Anna is practically dancing with excitement. "Are you girls heading out?" Anna begins with the same speech she gave to her Aunt at the fish shop. I grab her by the arm, and start pulling her slowly to the door.

The problem with giving my mother a story is you never know when she suddenly wants specifics. If she feels there is any gap in the story she will move into her FBI interrogation mode. Within a matter of minutes she will have found out our plan and completely put a stop to it, or worse; want to come along. Poor Anna doesn't stand a chance. My mom will have her unraveling like a skein of yarn.

"We are going to see the seals, and maybe get an ice cream." I add, as casually as I can. I can tell her curiosity is beginning to ignite. "Dad and I are going to take a walk later. Lets meet up. We will buy the ice cream." Anna looks slightly alarmed. I give my canned smile. "Sounds great, see you later." I push Anna towards the door with my body, not giving her any room, and shielding her face so my mother won't be able to read anything off it.

"How do you purpose we are going to be able to meet them for ice cream," Anna asks. Her voice sounding faintly defeated. "Don't sweat it Anna, it shouldn't take that long. We will get the seals to cooperate, because they want out of the busy harbor as much as we want them out, then we can head over and grab some ice cream. If it is taking a little longer to get through the tunnels, you can run over and tell them I am on the other side of the village helping them into the new basin." I pause questioning if Anna has what it takes to fool my mom. "Just don't let her think you are nervous, if she smells weakness, she will move in for the kill." She nods with a concerned look. I reassure her, even though I am not convinced.

Crossing the bridge, I am surprised to see that the traveller's camp is now abandoned. Even the tied horses are gone. The ground is torn up where the camper's once stood. Small piles of trash litter the broken earth. The earth scorched from a fire pit. Hard to believe this is where a group of families were living. I wonder what it must be like to just pack up your whole world and move in a few short days. Where did they go? Do they know themselves? Does one person make the call on when and where they move to, or do they come to some agreement? What about Mary, is she traveling in a caravan somewhere?

Anna's voice snaps me back. "Look there is Declan." I look down to see Declan on the temporary piers, with some lame looking tools, a flashlight, a tool belt, and a wagon. The boats in the harbor keep multiplying. Some jockey to get a slip while others just cruise the inlet, back and forth, up and down hoping someone will leave. Others are trying to double up.

This tangle of engines and crowds will make finding the seals difficult. I imagine the mayhem of the traffic has them in hiding. I only hope I can help them out.

As soon as Declan speaks, I can sense his vibe. He is overly anxious to get the mission underway. I can tell his mind is elsewhere again. I bet he has made other plans later. He probably wants to meet up with his girlfriend.

Hey, that suits me fine, because we need to find my parents. Lets face it. Those tunnels are disgusting. I would like to spend as little time as possible down there myself. As far as I am concerned we can't move fast enough.

It takes about ten minutes to figure out a way to attach the old metal cooler of fish carcasses onto the wagon, which is just slightly smaller. It is packed tight. Aunt Carol must have thought we were moving a whale.

The last thing we need is for the whole thing to spill on the cobblestone road. We all take a position on sides of the wagon, coaxing the lopsided wheels over the uneven stone pavement. Small sprays of fish sludge spill out and onto our hands and pants, as the wagon slowly rocks its way to the vent that will lead to the tunnel. "This will work out well. If we run out of fish the seals can just follow the scent off us." I give a half laugh, but my words fall on deaf ear. Anna is too busy looking around. She is nervous and Declan's mind is a million miles away. I am positive he is thinking about his secretive double life.

Arriving at the spot, Declan lowers first the ladder, and then himself toward the vent. Anna and I start throwing food. There is no sign of the seals. With all the traffic, it is hard to see anything. There are so many differing wakes, and ripples. "There, something silver." My eyes follow in the direction Anna's finger is pointing. The seals are moving in a slow line, barely swimming, more of just a float. I can't believe this is the same group that I have spent so much time with. There is no diving and skirting, absolutely no playfulness at all.

They move into the area and begin devouring the food. "Now that is more like it," I say, more for Anna's benefit; it doesn't take an expert to see that the seals aren't in great shape. They are nervous, constantly looking around, twitching and jumping with each passing boat engine. The color on most has dulled. Some seem listless, and the older seals push pieces of food at the smaller weaker ones, in an attempt to help them feed.

We pack bags of fish parts and neatly pile them up. Declan has opened the vent and bent it down enough so that he can sit on the edge. He gives the go ahead, and we start tossing the bags of food down to him. I throw one a little hard and it lands on the lip of the vent. Tearing the bag, it leaves a spray of fish carcasses oozing out and sticking to the vent. The seals' are so hungry they scurry around Declan's dangling legs, so close to him he could touch them. He looks up and gives a worried shrug. "They look awful, I don't think they would last much longer in the harbor, it is a good thing we are moving them." He looks at me with admiration. My face flushes, as I say, "lets hope they understand we are here to help."

When we have finished lowering the bulk of the food into the tunnels, I turn towards Anna. "You are going to be careful right? I want you to promise you will check for cars, before you stand over the grates." She grabs me and hugs me before she responds. "No bother, I'll be fine. Its you who needs to be mindful, please be careful Audrey." Declan calls from below.

I look over in just enough time to duck my head as a clunky piece of metal comes flying up. I reach out and grab it before it falls back into the water. Stretching my arms sends a painful reminding burn to my stomach where I injured myself on the boat. I look at what I just caught. It is a primitive radio thing. I am just about to ask what the heck, when I hear Declan's voice barely audible over the static. "Nice catch, over." I look over at Anna and roll my eyes, before I answer back. "Will we have to say over?" I pause for a second before adding, "Over."

I hand the walkie-talkie to Anna and wink at her before lowering myself down into the vent. Declan has removed most of the tools from the bag, and is busy strapping as much as he can to his belt. I look out at the seals that are just below us in the water. They look up at us, not the least bit afraid. I realize all those days of feeding them have made them trust me. I hope this is a wise decision on their part.

Picking up some bits of chopped fish from the vent wall, I can almost place them in an older seal's mouth, they are so trusting. I fight back the temptation to reach out and pet them.

We are suited up with all our supplies, which means we are considerably weighted down especially with all the bags of fish strapped all over our bodies. I have a tool belt with a flashlight and army knife. Declan will wait on the side of the vent while I try to persuade the seals to make the tiny leap up into the vent. There is enough water so the little ones can swim all the way through. We wait for the last bits of food to be eaten before we throw the food that will start the operation.

Declan will remain on the side of the vent until all the seals have come up, and then he will follow up the rear, making sure we are all together and accounted for. "Here goes nothing," I say opening the first bag and littering the murky water inside the main aqueduct. The water comes up to my shins and parts of many of the fish entrails swirl around my boots. A couple more inches of water and they would be able to slip inside.

The seals begin to jump onto the vent; some of the smaller ones linger a little before making the step. Just like us a couple of the larger ones stay behind and wait. We hope they will take up the rear of the procession. Once all the small ones are up and eating, the larger ones take the small leap.

I gasp as the last one jumps, or more like falls up onto the vent. His side has a massive wound, a huge gash oozing and crusty with old blood. It runs the length of his body. It looks as if he caught it on a rudder or engine blade. Although the salt water from the sea has helped the healing process, the gash runs so deep, I can see layers of his skin below. His coat is discolored and dull, he is moving so slowly, I am not sure if he will make it. "I don't know about this fella, he is hurt pretty badly." Declan says sadly as steps out behind the last seal, blocking their way, preventing them from heading back into the harbor.

The injured one turns and growls at Declan who quickly takes a step backward. "Sorry, not going hurt ya. I am just going to close the vent. I hope you guys aren't claustrophobic." Declan and I look at each other before I say, "I don't think they will attack us, but just to be on the safe side, we should make sure to give them some space." Declan agrees and takes out the radio. "We are in and good to go, Anna. We will let you know when we hit the first grate." He hesitates a minute after speaking. I think debating whether or not to say "over".

We start the slow march, strapped with bags of fish food, wearing a homemade carpenter's belt containing various tools, and trudging through an ancient glorified sewer, with a group of seals in a line between us. Declan must be realizing how absolutely ridiculous we look, because he lets out a laugh. It is so loud and from so deep in his belly, it comes out more of a howl. A few of the seals jump, in stunned surprise. The sound of his laugh echo in the hollow tunnels, and gives off an eerie reverberation. "We do look a sight." His voice sounds muffled and different, and maybe has a little fear mixed in. I am just glad we are underground. It is an added bonus to be able to lighten the load by throwing fish out of the bags.

It is a welcoming feeling to see the first grate ahead, and the last of the evening sun as it shines strong down through the metal. It makes a pattern of light. Beautiful prisms of colors dance on the top of the sludgy water giving off a fuzzy haze, a warm glow. I push my boots through the water; I will take it one grate at a time.

The sun pattern and warmth disappear and I am left with a feeling of sadness. A cold chill moves in. I reach over and grab the rope we have tied to the top of the grate. Pulling with my arms on the rope lightens some of the load from my feet. I look back at the group; the seals seem completely relaxed, eating fish with an obvious sense of relief to get out of the overpopulated harbor. Declan is trudging up the rear, pushing his weight through the water at a slow methodical pace, keeping his head down. I see the shadow of Anna through the grates. Everything is moving forward, to plan and I whisper to myself, "so far, so good."

We take a moment to regroup before pushing on. We are directly under the village, the place where old meets new. The most modern tunnels snake off of each side. It becomes noticeably darker. A strong stench of rotten food and car exhaust wafts through. I remember the smell of the death boats in my dream, which adds to the reeking odor, breathing into my sleeves offers only a short reprieve.

One of the seals lets out a defensive cry. A hairy mass rushes towards us in the water. Fear grabs hold of the animals as well as us. We scamper to the side of the sewer and push back. Declan's chest heaving, he looks for a tool to use as a weapon. The walls are circular, leaving no place to grab on. It is impossible to climb or scale. We are stuck. The injured seal bares his teeth, a hissing sound comes out, and he blocks the tunnel, protecting us. The creature swirls in circles as it approaches; as it comes in closer we get a full view. I place my hand over my mouth, holding in the throw-up that is ready to erupt.

It is a dead animal, probably a dog. Hard to tell what it was in life, because it is so bloated and decayed in death. Its open eye stare at us, the top of its head is wrapped in seaweed, giving an even more grotesque look. It rushes past and heads down one of the smaller more modern drains.

The faint, small voice of Anna comes crackling over the ancient radio, breaking the silence. Our bodies relax slightly. We both give an uncomfortable sort of laugh as we realize, there is in no imminent danger. "Lads, are you okay? Lads come in.... over." The transmission stops for a moment and then starts again, "Audrey, Declan I thought I heard a scream."

Declan pulls the radio from his belt, collects himself before responding, "No worries, Anna we are coming up on the second grate now." After my heart rate returns, I grab the rope and pull myself under the grate. A car passes over top. We are plunged into darkness for only a second before the sun returns. I hear the delicate steps of Anna's feet echoing above me, she is over the grate.

We push on into the darkest section, the underbelly of the village; the air is cold with moistness to it. It lands on our clothes and leaves a small wet spray. I finish throwing most of my bags full of fish and take a moment to rearrange the empty ones; I drop a bag and bend over to pick it up.

Through Declan's legs I see the immense wave. It quickens, and grows, swirling off the sides of the circular tunnel walls. Seaweed and debris are joining it, as it barrels towards us. I don't even have time to speak before it hits the back of his legs. Like a set of dominoes we all tumble. Declan hits the cement first. I hear the sound of snapping. It sounds like crisp celery being broken. The seals fly under me and I land on top of them. Like a football tackle we are piled, one on top of the other. The exception being Declan he is alone and floating. Face down. I rush to my feet. The wound on my stomach stings and burns, worse than when I first cut it. I stumble over the tools and supplies that have slipped off Declan's tool belt. My boots are heavy, weighted with water. I grab him by the scruff of his neck. He is so much heavier in the water. He is laying face down in the sludgy, sewer. Rolling him over, I see his face grimaced with pain. Semi-conscious he coughs up a mouthful of water. I lean him up against the side of the tunnel. The seals are floating everywhere. The neat and orderly procession in which we traveled is now gone. Some are in front, some are behind, and others just stand and stare, as if they too are recovering from the shock of the rogue wave.

Declan is definitely messed up, as to the extent of his injuries, it is hard for me to get a visual read on. The radio and most of his tools are gone. The seals gather themselves taking stock of the situation, far more adaptable then we are. Casually, a few begin to nibble the fish that is littered around. Most of Declan's fish bags are either punctured or ripped open. It is hard to tell if he is bleeding. He is spewing fish from all over. Again, with the fish guts, just like on the boat.

Fish guts and gills are mixed in with everything. I make an exaggerated gesture of pulling fish entrails off. I jokingly add, "Why does this keep happening?" My humor is definitely lost on him. He is favoring his arm, keeping it tucked in close to his body, making it difficult to see. What I know to be true is that he is messed up. I am pretty certain arms aren't supposed to bend that way. "I think you may have broken your arm. Does it hurt anywhere else?" He looks up before answering, " I think the better question to ask would be where doesn't it hurt?" He tries to sound casual, but its obvious he is in pain.

Collecting all the bags, I begin tying them together. I also try to lighten the mood. "Sure, we capsize a boat in the harbor, and we end up with a couple of scrapes. Today we are leveled by a two foot sewer surge." He tries to smile as I create a makeshift sling out of the empty rotting fish bags. That are littered around. Turning towards him, I am alarmed by what I see; he looks as if a train has hit him. If I weren't bent over, I would probably be in the same shape. Aside from the throbbing, burning pain in my stomach, I feel pretty good. I hold up my knotted collection of bags, wiping off any excess fish entrails. "I think we should try to tie up your arm. It is bent backwards, so I may need to slide it a little then I will tie this on."

He is trying to be brave and I am trying to be gentle, but the truth of the matter is we are in way over our heads. I take a moment to access our situation. Declan needs medical attention. We are too far into the tunnels to head back; we have a group of seals that will need rounding up. Anna is wandering the roads above us. And I am scared, really scared.

The seals begin to circle around us clearing the area of any fish parts. I get the sling onto Declan's shoulder; it is a temporary fix. What he needs is to have his arm set properly by a hospital. We agree that I should head onto the next grate. I won't tell Anna the extent of our accident, but I will let her know. We will be moving considerably slower. I untie the fish bags and pile them next to Declan. All the bait spilled out so it won't be necessary for him to continue to carry them. I find the flashlight floating along and pick it up. It sputters light for a second and then goes completely black. I grab a bag that is floating by, and begin picking up any of our stuff that I come across. My body is wrecked. It takes every bit of strength I have to push on. Some of the seals follow me for a few paces, then double back to stay with the group and feed. I get one last look at Declan, who considering the circumstances, is resting sort of comfortably. He looks to be almost enjoying all the attention of the seals.

The sun is fading and the tunnels are getting darker by the minute. I hear Anna's voice frantically calling us. I swing my arms and grab the rope, pulling with all my might. I land directly below her on the grate. "Sorry about that, we lost our radio, and took a bit of a tumble." Luckily she cuts me off before I have to give her too many details. "Captain McMahon is here, and he is looking for Declan. He is really cross. I also saw your parents, and well I didn't know what to say, so I sort of ran away. I think they are looking for us on the other side of the village." Oh great, can this night get any worse? It takes everything I have not to drop down in the dirty water and cry.

All right, what to do, what to do? I once again compose myself before I call up to her. "We are more than halfway. Lets just get this done. It will take my parents a while before they think to look on this side of the village. Stay out of sight. Wait at the vent opening, we won't check in at the grates, its too risky. Someone might see you standing in the road, talking to the sewer."

I turn and begin the walk back to Declan. I am debating whether to tell him about his father. Seeing the look of pain and discomfort on his face, I decide to tell him after we get out of here. He needs all the strength he has, no need having him worry about his Dad. Besides once his father sees his arm, how mad will he be? Parents forget that other stuff when they see you're injured.

The last passage lies ahead. The seals travel with us back in formation and completely comfortable. They weave and skirt between our legs making our steps even slower. No longer weighted down by the tools is somewhat of help, but the weight of Declan's pain is a far heavier burden.

Declan's face grimaces with each step. I begin to see daylight from the vent. "Look, we are almost there." I try to sound optimistic. The walkway path begins to appear, growing wider as it winds towards the makeshift door. I slow my pace to grab hold of his good arm. I help push him up the small incline. I scamper up behind him and pull open the door.

A blast of pink evening sky nearly knocks me off my feet. Declan steadies on the wall next to the door. I am about to climb back to try to release the final vent. The seals block my path; they scurry up the side and cluster together at the doorway.

One nudges Declan's hand, while another sticks his body out the door and hesitates for just a moment, before leaping into the surf below. One by one the seals follow. It is as if they know. A few slow for a last look back. Staring at me as if to memorize my face. I feel a slight tear, not a sad tear, but a proud happy one; a strong feeling of pride rushes through. I look to Declan.

I am about to speak when he smiles, he nods his head with a complete understanding of what I am feeling.

The last seal, the older one with the large cut on his side stands at the doorway, he looks below to all the seals frolicking in the open, peaceful sea inlet. "I hope you will be okay? I will never forget you." He stares at me. I know he understands every word I just said, after a while, he thrusts his body forward and propels himself into the air. He dives and is gone into the blue green water below.

I hear a cheer from above us. I lean out the door and look towards the sound. Anna is jumping and cheering as she sees the seals playing in the safe water below. I stick my fist up in the air. "We did it." I shout up. She yells back, in agreement.

Declan is moving towards me at a slow and steady pace. He looks a wreck, his clothes are covered in muddy fish parts, splattered with bloodstains. His arm is wrapped in torn plastic bags; each one carries its own wretched fish odor. I push him up the path and Anna grabs him from above. She heaves him over the last of the hill and onto the street above. I turn and grab as many of the tools as I can see. I trudge through the dark tunnel collecting some that are floating towards us. The rest I can come back for, after they have had a chance to float down. Although the idea of coming back to these dark, stinky tunnels is not something I am looking forward to.

I pull the last of the tools, and myself up to the road. We embrace in a stinky bear hug. Anna tries hard to hold us, but I can tell she is grossed out by our stench. I grab a huge piece of fish guts stuck on my pants and put my hand out to her. "Here, I got this for you." I say as I proudly present her with it. "Very funny, I have been worried sick about you, what took so long?" She asks as she knocks the mess from my hand.

Before we begin the walk across the village; we take a moment to watch the seals. They frolic and play peacefully in the sea below. We stand united, feeling tranquil and proud.

Heading back at a slow pace so Declan can keep up, we listen to the rattle of the old wagon across the stone. I still feel tingly from the accomplishment. The planning, the training, the research, amazing, it all came together. Nothing can wreck this evening. I open my mouth to share my victorious feeling. Before I have a chance to say anything Anna turns towards Declan and says, "I think your father is still at the pier, he was really in a state." Declan stops dead in his tracks; I have never seen him look so frightened. "Did you say Dad is at the pier?" Anna nods sheepishly.

The mood changes instantaneously. Declan begins moving in larger strides, sort of limping and jogging at the same time. He is moving like the zombies walk in those cheesy horror movies. Even his eyes seemed kind of bulgy. After every few steps he lets out a labored sigh or a almost inaudible "No, please." At first I try to console him. "Look, it will be fine, I can go back first thing in the morning and get the rest of the tools. Just explain, he will understand. It was for a good cause. Won't he be glad we got the seals out of his harbor?" I try everything, I am becoming winded trying to talk and keep up with him. At this point, he is almost in a full run. "It's not like anything got broken, its just a little wet, we can dry it." I notice his agitation is growing with every over sized step he takes. He finally yells back at me with hatred in his voice. "You don't get it," he breaks into a full run.

Anna has fallen far behind and the wagon I am pulling begins to clank with the few tools I was able to save, randomly hitting the pavement. My feelings are so hurt, and with the weight of exhaustion, I begin to do what I least want to be doing. I tear up. "Whatever." I scream out towards the direction Declan went. "How are you even moving that quickly, I had to practically pull you out of the tunnel?"

Anna catches up to me and helps refill the wagon. I busy myself with collecting the fallen tools, pretending to be securing each on onto the wagon, so Anna doesn't see how angry and hurt I am. We straighten ourselves out and walk in silence.

Rounding the corner we can see Davis, Declan's father. He is shaking something; it looks to be a tarp. Coming closer reveals it to be a person. He is violently shaking someone by the neck; a head is bobbing back and forth. Declan is running over and screaming. I can hear him yelling. "Stop it." The rest I can't quite make out. I turn toward Anna, and with complete panic in my voice I yell. "Go, get help." Before I even finish the sentence, she turns and runs towards the center of the village.

For a few steps I continue to push the wagon, more out of shock. Finally dropping the handle, it scrapes across the cobblestone road, rolling alongside me for a few strides, before it topples over.

Davis has thrown aside the person he was originally choking, the body lies in a small heap on the dock, and he turns his full fury towards Declan. The hatred in his stare stops me midway on the steps. He is walking slowly towards Declan. "Or what, what are you going to do? You... I could crush you with one hand." His arm flexes. His muscles bulge in a grotesque shape that slithers up his arm. Declan seems to deflate, he cowers for only a second and then he stands tall, his shoulders roll back, he grows another few inches before my eyes. He tears the plastic sling off and clenches his fists.

"Enough Dad, its over. I am not afraid of you anymore." His words resonate, and strong. Davis stops for only a second.

"You better be lad, you think you are protecting her." He points to the crumpled up mass. "She doesn't care about you. She left you. He spits out another insult. "I am all you have, without me, you have nothing." He punches Declan in the stomach. Declan bends over, clutching his stomach. He stays hunched over before he half raises himself. He runs straight at Captain Davis and buries his head into his stomach. They fall backwards a few paces; someone lets out a painful groan.

I hear my own voice. "Stop it right now, Declan. Captain you stop this right now." They seem to slow, a moment of clarity, pushing away from each other. Declan spins and is facing me. Pulling himself tall he stares in silence. Captain Davis straightens himself and stands, his back is too me. He directs himself to Declan. "How dare you touch me."

A voice behind speaks, clear and soft but strong. "Davis you are done brutalizing my family. You have hit my sister and my nephew for the last time." Deidre steps down the stairs, she is holding Anna's hand. Davis begins to turn slowly. "What do you think you are going to do about it?" His evil menacing face begins to melt. A frightened look crosses.

I turn around to see what has him scared. Standing along the road, on the pier, on the steps, on the jetty, everywhere I look, there are people. I see my parents, Aunt Carol and Uncle Joe from the fish shop, the people from the pub, the people from the bakery, the people from the library. Everyone I have ever met, since I arrived, and a bunch of people I don't know. Even the man who hit us with his boat and his wife, I mean everyone. My parents push past the crowd and climb down the stairs to rest their hands on my shoulders.

The one thing all these people have in common is where they are looking. They are all looking at Captain Davis; no they are glaring at him. I can't even imagine what that must feel like, to have that much hatred directed at you. He looks down right terrified.

Declan and Deidre race over to the crumpled figure and help her stand to her feet. They are hugging. Davis pushes himself farther down the pier. He has no escape but he still steps backwards slowly. A few more steps and he will fall off the end of the pier and into the dark ocean.

"You are through here, I want you off my dock and out of my marina, you are fired. I don't ever want to see the likes of you again." It's the man from the pub, the stout bartender, standing with his hands on his hips, his apron tied around his waist. Davis squints his eye. The dark car that picked up Declan the other night pulls up to the pier screeching to a halt. The man with blond kinky hair, the man I have seen driving jumps out.

He takes the steps two at a time. He is carrying paperwork in his hand. He runs to Declan and the woman. He whispers to them, his face covered in concern. He turns slowly towards Davis.

The tall stranger with the kinky hair and wire-rimmed glasses clears his throat. Davis takes one look at this man who is physically much smaller. He puffs himself up a bit, regaining some of the bravado that was taken from him by the people that have witnessed his brutality.

The man tries to appear calm; he takes a breath and pushes his glasses up. Davis takes a step towards him trying to pull back on his bullying mask. He clenches his fists and moves invading this man's space.

There is a second of silence before the man speaks, "I won't fight you with my fists. I will fight you with something much stronger. I will fight you with the law. I can have you thrown into jail right now; I have enough witnesses to make a case against you." The crowd lets off a cheer. Anna's Uncle Joe steps forward, "I got an even better idea. I say we take justice into our own hands. I say we give Captain Davis what he deserves. We handle this our own way." The crowd begins cheering and moving towards the pier steps. Davis steps back.

The crowd grows even angrier, there is a rumbling. This must be how a mob mentality forms. After witnessing the violent act, they are gathering strength amongst themselves. They are appalled at what they have witnessed from this man.

Declan steps forward and raises his arm. "Stop, STOP. He is still my Dad. Please leave him be." That sends an immediate silence through the crowd. A voice, maybe even my father's is heard, "The boy is right, there has been enough violence already. Please, let this be the end." A hush falls over the group. Deidre and the woman whisper, the man with the glasses walks over, he listens. He walks towards Declan; gently he lays his hand on his shoulder. "Wise words from a good man, thank you Declan." He says proudly.

The man with the kinky hair moves towards Captain Davis, he stares at him. "Let me get a feel for your situation: you were seen by all these witnesses committing an act of violence against a woman and a boy. You have been fired from your job, and asked to leave the premises. These fine citizens are ready to beat you into next week. I think it might be time for you to consider relocating. I hear the other side of Ireland is lovely." Again, the crowd breaks into applause and cheering.

Captain Davis looks as if he might say something. His mouth is about to form words. He looks around taking a moment to take it all in. "All the hell, with you all." This sends the crowd into another roar of applause. He slowly climbs the steps to the pier. The crowd opens to give him a clear path. Everyone watches as he slowly walks off.

I turn towards my parents and we hug. My mother takes a long look at me. She shakes her head as she sees the ragged clothes, the dried fish blood, and then smells the awful stench. "Audrey, are you okay? Did that monster hurt you?"

I laugh before I answer. "No Mom, this happened before. We were working with the seals. They are free." I pause for a moment. "It's a long story, can I tell you tomorrow?" She looks at me; her worried look falls away, replaced with love in her eyes. "Of course honey."

Anna runs over to us, and begins tugging on my arm. I look down and smile, "Anna, you rock. When I told you to get help, I never imagined you would bring the whole village." My parents smile, too. She shrugs her shoulders. "I didn't know who to get, so I just brought everyone." She waits, checking to make sure I wasn't disappointed by her decision before she says, "Come over here, I want you to meet my Aunt Mary." We start moving towards the group, but there is a swarm of people surrounding them. "Can we maybe meet her later?" Anna looks disappointed until I point out, "she has a lot of old friends who want to say hello." Anna agrees, and before my parents and I head back, my mom stops a minute and looks downward, "I love her shoes." she gloats. I immediately recognize them from the other night; Mary was the mystery woman Declan was coming to meet. The one I saw him hugging. The one he kept leaving us for. I smile and nod. It has been a long day and I am exhausted. Between moving the seals, and all the adventure, I can't wait to take a shower and go to sleep. I catch Declan's eye in the crowd, and I give a small wave. He smiles back and waves.

Chapter 18

I lift my shirt in the mirror to look at my wound. The soreness follows the red outline and now is swollen. Carefully, I dab it with a warm washcloth. I am too tired to go find my mother. I opt to deal with it in the morning.

I barely remember climbing into bed. The room seems so warm. I am dizzy. Tossing and turning, warm wet hair sticks to my face. Dreams come and go, not nearly as realistic as before.

The castle is dark, there are torches outside and I am upstairs. Trapped in bed, my body too heavy to lift. I hear Vivian. Her voice is muffled. There is a flurry of activity and I hear horses hooves and loud voices. There is an intruder. But why are the ravens silent?

I wake back in the blue bedroom at the top of the stairs in our rental house. The raven's shadow circles my bedspread. Faster and tighter the bird is spiraling above, circling outside the skylight, above my head. The shadow of the full wingspan grows larger as it comes closer, covering the bed and me. Round and round it circles. Tighter and tighter still, the sound is shatteringly loud. CAAAHHH!! I sit up; the sheets are knotted and tangled. I have been tossing and turning so much the bed is totaled.

What happened at the castle? It was dangerous and something was amiss. I sit on the end of my bed cradling my forehead. It is so sore, and it burns. Hot to the touch. I am so confused, my heart racing, my head pounding. I scream back at the raven, "I did what you asked, I helped them, the seals are safe. What more do you want from me?"

The sound of paws scratching on the thick pine planks outside the bedroom door, a sniffing. The door opens. Anna is there with a black fluffy puppy attached to her arm with a thin rope. His paws are four sizes bigger than his body, he constantly trips over them when he lumbers in whimpering.

"Audrey look, this is my new dog, Mum says I can keep him. I am going to call him Bear. Mary brought him from Dublin." Her voice is filled with excitement. Her words spilling out so fast, I find it hard to understand her. My head is pounding. "Mom says we need a man around the house." She pauses for a moment, "You don't look good, are you okay?" I mumble and nod before attempting to stand up.

"Mary, Mary will know, yes." I need to talk to Mary. I turn towards Anna, who is looking at me with a questioning expression, her head slightly turned. "Audrey, are you okay?"

I make a quick stop at the mirror. "Yikes," I bellow. One look at me from Mom and I will be bed-bound for sure. I do look bad, not half as bad as I feel. I will be unable to hide this from Inspector Mom. I am going to need help with this. I look towards Anna, a bundle of smiles with her new puppy. She looks up concerned. "Look, I nearly forgot. We are having a party up at the house and Granny is fixing a feast. Mary and her friend, and Declan, and Mum, you and your parents, and me and Bear, everyone is going. Come on we can head over."

I slink down the last set of stairs, quickly poking my head in the kitchen. Mom is busy preparing to bring something to Granny's party. I move while her back is turned, gliding through the kitchen, my back to her heading towards the glass doors. A few more steps and I will be through. Anna and Bear trudge loudly behind; Bear yanks hard on the small piece of rope Anna has tied to him. He makes a panting, choking sound. His paws click along the kitchen tile.

My mother yells to me over my shoulder, "Audrey, you are awake, its almost noon. Where are you going?" I think fast, "UUmmm, Granny needs some help getting ready for the dinner. She sent Anna to get me. I need to go." There is no way my mother is going to stop me from helping. "Well what about breakfast?" I quickly push out the door, holding it long enough for Anna to pass through. Before I answer, "I will grab something, I promise, thanks Mom see you up at the house." With that I am gone. Anna has to run to keep pace. Bear, tripping over his enormous paws, side stepping behind, loves the chase game. Even if he is being half dragged by his leash.

"Sorry, about that Anna, but I need to speak to Mary right away." Anna confused, but glad to have me around smiles and shrugs. The fresh air feels good on my flushed skin. I take in huge breaths of it. I try to push out the bad air. This causes my head to pound worse, now I have a massive headache.

As soon as I enter the house, I recognize Mary immediately. It is hard to get her alone for a conversation, because everyone at the old manor house is surrounding her; everyone wants to be part of the celebration and in great spirits. It feels like we have slain a dragon. There is a real sense that Mary is back and Davis is gone, and peace is once again restored to this land. I look over at Mary, too bad that can't be said for Vivian's land.

Mary catches my glance. Her petite figure tenses for a moment. Her pale eyes stare back at me. The group chatters on, loudly and happily around us. We look at each other, an unspoken moment. Desperate to speak to her, I will have to find the patience to wait for the right moment.

I meet her lawyer friend, the thin man at the pier. He also was the driver from the car that kept appearing to mysteriously pick up Declan. His name is Brian and he is far more than just her attorney. This is easy to spot by the way he looks at her. I would say he is crazy about her. She is a beautiful woman, her thick dark hair frames a narrow face, and her pale eyes are caught between gorgeous shades of blue and green. Her features are so perfect, she reminds me of someone I would see in a magazine selling clothes.

At each person's arrival, a small re-celebration begins. Once again, Grandma has out done herself. We sit down to a feast. Each platter is passed around at least once. Mary's story of her last five years begins to come out. She was never in a traveller's camp. That was just a rumor Davis started. The people, who love her, let it go, to keep him off the track of finding her.

She has been studying in Dublin and now has a degree in of all things, history. I guess in the process she met Brian. It seems everyone but Davis knew where Mary was, including Grandma. I am shocked she had not mentioned it. The table is a huge square filling most of the dining room. Sitting across from Mary makes it impossible to start a private conversation. I am able to watch her, study her for any clues or signs any presence of Vivian or acknowledgement of who I am. My parents are seated far enough away that they have no clue that I am not feeling well.

Mary stands and begins collecting plates that are finished. She carries the load out the door and down the hall to the kitchen. I quickly collect as many as I can. Trying to catch a moment alone with her. My father holds his plate ready to serve himself a third helping. I grab it out of his hand and exit quickly.

She is standing at the sink with her back towards me. Finally I have a chance alone with Mary. Where do I start? What do I say? After a long breath for courage, I begin, " I love your drawings Catherine Mary."

She shuts off the sink, slowly methodically she turns. She takes a moment, a quiet small laugh or sigh, passes before she starts, " I had a feeling it was you. It has taken me fifteen years and countless hours of therapy to convince myself that the castle, Vivian, all of it was nothing more than dreams. Just a fairy tale, made up by a sad girl who needed justification." She dries her hand on a towel, when I ask, "justification for what?" She slowly answers, "I don't know for what.... for finding the treasure, maybe?" She rests the towel on the counter before looking at me and saying. "When I saw you at the pier last night, all doubt vanished. I recognized you immediately, my sister Freya. Vivian's courageous youngest daughter, you have been in so many of my dreams."

It feels as if someone had pushed me back. All the air from my chest is suddenly being grabbed and yanked out. I am speechless. I can't believe I have been in her dreams, as she has been in mine. How can this be? I collect myself and prepare to blast her with questions; only the kitchen fills with people carrying piles of dishes and napkins, all the spoils from the meal. They step between us.

My mother takes one look at my face and stops, "Audrey, are you okay?" Before I have a chance to answer, Anna and Bear pass through, "Audrey come quick, I want to show you what I taught Bear. He can climb through a tunnel. He is brilliant." I smile fondly. "Yeah great. I would love to see." I smile at my Mom.

This time Mary chimes in and my mother turns to her. "If its is okay, maybe Audrey could spend the night? We have so much in common. She loves history as much as I do. I would love to show her some of my drawings?" I add, "Please Mom? Mary knows so much about the history around here, please can I stay?" My mother is reluctant, she is about to walk over and put her hand on my head. I dodge around and scoop up Bear, as kind of a block, "I need to see how truly talented this guy is anyway." This gets Anna all excited again. My mother is clearly out numbered and is forced to relent. "Audrey, you look about my size, I can give you some pajamas." Mary adds, clinching the deal. My Mom can't say no.

Anna is begging, bribing, and eventually pushing Bear through the make shift tunnel she made out of a blanket and two boxes. I nod approvingly, but my mind is miles, or should I say centuries away.

I wander towards the library. I can hear Anna still trying to convince Bear to go through, his belly bloated from all the treats she has given him.

I move Declan's drawings to the side, giving room to spread out Mary's. I pull one of Vivian up close to see if I can see a resemblance.

This is ridiculous; I am not even from here. I am an average American girl here for the summer. This can't be. I feel her standing at the doorway. I can tell it is Mary. I have to admit, there is a connection with this woman, with this whole family, for that matter. "What happened to Vivian?" I ask.

She gracefully walks in, putting her hand on my shoulder; she pauses, preparing for what she will say next. "They killed her, Audrey." The shock and pain almost overbearing, I whisper, "What?" She adds, "They hanged her from the maple tree that stands near the vegetable garden." Another shock, I step backward. "What, who the soldiers, the crew from the death ships? Who killed her? Mary, my dreams they are scattered. Please help me, I need to put it together." Her voice broken and terrified, "I will try to help you. That horrible night that Vivian died was the last dream for me. It was the last time I stepped foot in that realm Audrey."

Chapter 19

Mary collects her drawings, she moves to the overstuffed chairs, motioning me to the one across from her. My body drops with a heavy heart and a pounding head. I sit ready to hear. I know this isn't going to be a happy tale. I need to hear it anyway.

Mary starts by saying that her dreams also, were fragmented. Out of time, out of sequence, and definitely missing parts, and filled with gaps. She has had a lot more dreams than I. With her history studies, she has been able to piece some parts together. With that taken into consideration, there still is a lot of speculation. Having to fill in the blanks based on what she has learned in history, not what she has seen, or lived, or whatever you call these dreams her and I share.

She starts with the castle. She thinks illness killed most. Vivian and a few others survived. The village and church soon cut all ties with the outside world. They barricaded themselves behind the city walls, a feeble attempt to keep the illness out.

Its not clear who Vivian was, or what her part at the castle was when it was prosperous. Was she a serf, or from the lord's family? How or who survived the illness is unclear but Mary is convinced they suffered from what was most likely the plague.

It is not long after that time the poor and weak villagers go missing. Rumor's and folklore run rampant. All outsiders are immediately under suspension. Naturally the castle, high on the cliffs, is an easy target. No one will venture up to find out, everyone is convinced it is the source of the sickness. Rumors are that spirits and madness rule, and anyone who enters pledges their soul to the underworld.

Mary shows me the drawings of the pirate ships. We have both had the unfortunate experience of witnessing them waiting just outside the harbor. We have helped Vivian rescue as many of the sold slaves as we could. They trolled the coast just like the fishing boats do today.

I can't even imagine being on a ship for years, stopping at ports along the way up the coasts, possibly over land, from as far as the Middle East or the coast of Africa.

The crew would plunder the fleets when possible, stealing cargo. Sometimes all a boat had aboard to plunder, was crew, so that meant taking people. They needed slaves to work the plantations or to sell. When they can't get the bodies they need from forcibly taking the ships, then they look to the shores.

If they can't get enough human cargo from the other boats or near the shore, then they look elsewhere." The shock and horror of Mary's words makes me sick. The same way I felt when I learned about the slave trade in America. How can people deal in human cargo?

I feel vomit rise in my throat, my head pounds, what it must have been like to have your family taken from you. "Oh Mary, I can't even imagine how desperate you would have to be to sell your family, or even a stranger for that matter." Mary shakes her head. " But they were, and they did, for whatever reasons. Many turned to the black market. Bartering and buying with the only commodity they had. Dealing in human trade. The buyers are resourceful, having traveled far; they need to fill their ships. To justify the journey before heading back. There is no profit in bringing a ship that is only half full back, so they take when and what they can to meet their quotas."

We both shake our heads in disgust. We have experienced the destruction first hand of these barbaric business dealings. Seen the brutality and pain caused by these death ships.

Mary adds. "What the villagers don't know is that the very ships that they sell their people to were very well the same ships that brought the plague to them. Many say the plague that desecrated most of Europe came from a flea from the Orient. The flea attached itself to the black rat that also traveled far on the ships, all the way to the European shores, a deadly stow - away spreading disease up the coasts."

Mary and I trade stories about what we have seen, where we travel in our sleep. Piecing together our dreams to fill in the gaps that the history books have left unwritten. We both have seen the soldiers. We have seen with our own eyes, the boats rowing towards the death ships with the people they have kidnapped in the village. Bound and tied, their cargo ready to be sold.

The villagers are led to believe its some evil spirit. Vivian and her black magic have taken their loved ones in the night. The few that follow the boats, the only witness to the soldier's deeds, are either killed on the spot or banished from the walled village. Left to fend for themselves outside the gates, where they are unable to share their stories. Because of Vivian's defense systems, there would be no going to her castle for shelter. Besides they are still convinced the castle is the epicenter for the disease that kills so mercilessly.

I ask Mary, "what about the woods surrounding the castle? There must have been people who were witness to what happened. There must be camps of people out there, right?" Mary responds, "I don't know Audrey, communication was non - existent during those times.

In its place there was speculation, illness and starvation."

I remember Miss Perkins history class; she said that Irish folk tales and lore were huge. I imagine the stories alone would cause a lot of paranoia and hysteria, as well. No wonder everyone was so afraid of Vivian. People need a reason for why bad things happen, a scapegoat. It sounds like Vivian was theirs. Mary repeats a saying. I have heard my mother say. "Paranoia breeds contempt." Which means when people are afraid and unsure they turn on each other.

Those were dark days for sure. Mary grows increasingly sadder as she speaks of her time with Vivian. I wonder where she was for the hanging? Where was I?

She seems to be winding up, coming to the end. She has had many more dreams than I. If I lived here, in Ireland longer than a summer, would the dreams continue to come? Mary doesn't speak of the night Vivian was killed. Instead she dances around this topic. The truth of what she saw on the night Vivian died is far too raw. She seems confused. My own dreams come in fragmented memories out of sequence; some are fuzzy while some are crystal clear.

She takes me back to the night. The last night she saw Vivian. Her voice breaks and she stops to collect for a moment before she speaks. This is incredibly painful for her. The actual events surrounding Vivian's death are sketchy. She begins to tell the story, to the best of her recollection. Her face grimaced, her eyes filled with tears. Her voice, so eloquent earlier, now cracking and faltering. I grasp her hand. It is obvious she needs to tell this story. She needs it to be heard, she begins again." Vivian and I were around the kitchen hearth. The evening was cold. We heard the yells along with the pounding of hooves in the courtyard. Vivian told me to run into the woods. I said no. I wouldn't go, she begged, she said there wasn't time. She promised me she would come and get me, she swore she would; she said she recognized the voices. She knew the horse; it was the blacksmith. That is why the ravens fell silent. They had traded before. She trusted him.

Only it wasn't the man she knew, this man was wild with rage. He was with his son. His young daughter had gone missing. An old woman in the village had told him that Vivian had taken her. She said she saw it in the smoke. She read the message in the fire that the flame sent her. She said it was Vivian, she told of a sacrifice she saw. Vivian performed one she swore. The old woman told him that Vivian had given his daughter to the devil himself.

Vivian yelled and began her ranting. I think she was having one of her fits. She tried to defend herself, but she was no match. They caught her off guard. She trusted him. The man was beside himself; he seemed to be touched in the head like Vivian. A rope was thrown around her neck. They galloped around the court. Huge draft horses pounded the earth, dragging her body across the ground. The rope taut, she could no longer speak. The ravens become alarmed and began to take flight. They flew in a tight circle around. But the men were ready for this. They were almost expecting it. They threw tarps over the flock and began trampling them with their horses and with Vivian, as she was being dragged behind them. Their torches burned, they stopped under the tree, that lines the vegetable garden."

Mary is riddled with fear and remorse. She grabs my arm, her face covered in panic fear and guilt. "I tried to help her Audrey, I swear to you, I really did. I wanted to run out. Shoot my arrow but I couldn't, I was stuck. My feet wouldn't move. I was no longer in the dream. I was merely watching, a nightmare. I was powerless to help, they pulled her up right there, high in the tree before my very eyes." With that Mary's head drops, her body limb, she reminds me of a piece of glass that is shattered and broken.

The room begins to spin, the heat in my head feels as if it will explode off my shoulders. "Mary," that is all I can say. I hear her voice. "You are burning up." I fade in; I manage to tell her I don't feel very well. I vaguely remember going into a guest room.

After that it's foggy. I lay in bed, a cool compress is across my forehead. I open my crusty eyes. My voice barely a whisper, "is it the plague, the black death?" Vivian smiles. " Shh, It is okay my darling, you will be fine." She holds a ladle of water for me. I am too sick to drink. I lay back on the soft feathery pillow. I drift in and out of sleep, sometimes I see Catherine Mary, sometimes Vivian.

Chapter 20

The dreams come at me, quickly fading in and out in montage form. Some are quiet and peaceful. Others are dark and threatening.

We are climbing up the hill, carrying the heavy sacks cradled on our hips. It is a beautiful day. The sky is a lovely blue, the billowy clouds slowly move across. We are so proud of our garden, as we enter the small walled yard. We place the sacks of seaweed onto the ground.

I am in front of the great hearth; I walk with the ladle, spooning watery gruel to the people huddled and shivering. That is when I notice her, the small child sitting by the fire. She is trying to hide. She is covered in fear. I reach to cradle her, she cowers and closes her eyes tightly. "It is okay, I won't hurt you. You are safe now." I whisper softly to her. She is so frightened. "Who is your father, is he the blacksmith?" I ask as she stares at me mutely.

I run outside to the old stable where the horse we traded for stands. He nervously stamps his feet while I dig in the dirty straw, fumbling with my fingers until I find what I need. The metal cold to my touch, I run back to the hearth. I find the small child arms wrapped around her knees, she is tucked into a tight ball. Trying to disappear into herself.

I lift the horseshoe. I point. "Your father?" She looks at me, she doesn't understand, "I lift my arm in an attempt to look like I am forging a shoe. She cowers farther into her tiny ball. She thinks I am going to strike her. "No. No." I say shaking my head. I act like a blacksmith, a primitive sort of sign language, and then I move around and pretend to rock a baby." She understands, and nods. "Da tt ddy..." a guttural sound, but she definitely knows what I am asking.

A new dream bleeds over the old. We are back in the garden emptying the bags; carefully we begin to place the seaweed on top of the vegetables, the salty dew from the still drying weeds sticks on my lips. Vivian smiles at me, "Eyee, we shall have a beautiful harvest now." She is so proud. She sings in a lovely soft voice.

My dreams skip and jump around, one minute we are gardening and frolicking outside, the next we are desperate, hiding and cold.

It is dark now, the room is so cold and someone sits near me. "Who is there?" I cry out. My voice is beaten down by fever. "Ring around the rosy, a pocket full of posies...." I hear the crackled voice of a small child who is rocking back and forth, a burlap bag cut at the middle dangles over her.

"Who...?" Is all I can say. She is so thin with big dark black circles under her eyes. She rocks back and forth. I recognize her; we took her from the death ships. The blacksmith's daughter sings a haunting tune while I lie in my bed with death whispering in my ear.

"Achoo, Achoo, we all fall down." She keeps singing the song over and over. She stares down at me; my body lays on the feather bed in the cold dark room, ravaged by the sickness. She is in a cationic state, rocking back and forth. Staring at me, her mind gone. I pity this little child. After all she has been through. Will she have to witness my death as well? A cough deep down rattles my chest. Warmth for a moment, then burning heat travels up into my throat.

I hear the sound of horses and screaming. I try to stand. I am too weak. The child, I yell to her," Go downstairs, show yourself, it's your father." She is deafened by the horrors of what she has been through. She sits and rocks back and forth, looking directly into my eyes she softly sings. "We all fall down."

I wake to Mary sitting at my bedside, "Audrey, you are awake, I am worried you have a fever. I need to call your mother. You have been tossing and turning." I sit up and grab her hand, "There is no time to call my mother. I found the blacksmith's daughter; you need to help me, because we need to show him. We have to tell him, she is upstairs in the castle."

Mary stares at me looking frightened, but curious enough to will me to continue. "Mary, on the night he comes, his daughter is upstairs. She is sitting with me." Mary looks confused. "You can't call my mother now, we have to go back in the dreams, me and you. We have to save Vivian and the little girl, and the blacksmith, it's a terrible misunderstanding." She looks really freaked out. "You, why do I have to save you, you just have a fever?" I sit up frantic, "You don't have to save me, you have to save them, you have to help me right this wrong." Before I can say more. The death rattle cough starts in my chest. This time the voice that comes from my throat is not my own, it has an accent " NO Catherine, you won't be helping me, I can't be helped." She looks more confused then ever, so I speak slower. "You can't help me, because I have the plague."

Mary looks to me with complete shock. "Of course you don't have the plague, luv." I start slowly, how can I explain? I don't even really understand it myself. "Mary, in my dream. I am sick. Vivian's daughter or Freya, who is me... We need to go back..." Mary interrupts me, "Audrey, I haven't been back in the dreams. When Vivian died that was my last dream, it is over." With that she puts her head down, she whispers in defeat. "You can't change the past."

I fall back on the pillow, my headache pounds through my head all the way to my teeth. It can't be the end. We have been dragged into these dreams for some reason. We certainly aren't meant to sit back and watch this happen. In Mary's case for a second time, no way, there must be more, if I could just think, "Mary wait, Vivian sent me a message, she passed through. She was telling me to help the seals. I know that is what she was saying. She was helping me. Look at all these dreams. She is here. Her spirit is anyway. We have to do something."

Mary's shoulders roll slightly back, her posture straightens. "But the dreams they have ended for me. I can't go back even if I want to."

My head is rattling, pounding a hammer behind my forehead. Chiseling away from the inside, out. My chest from the injury on the boat throbs. How easy it would be to just go home and rest. We are leaving in a few days; I could just head back to the states and forget this awful mess. But something stops me. I can't walk away. I have to try and do something.

"I got it." I say it so loudly. I startle myself. " The dreams, my dreams anyway, they come to me out of sequence. They are fading. Getting near the end. Almost gone. We can go back, back to the beginning, the time in the dreams that are happier. We could try alerting Vivian. For starters we could tell her that the mute girl is the blacksmith's daughter. We have to do something. We must warn the blacksmith, bring him his daughter, something." This seems like a long shot, I am saying this plan aloud trying to recruit Mary to help me, but deep down, I don't necessarily believe it. I have to try anyway. Pushing doubt aside isn't easy, but I have to try. I owe it to Vivian.

"The castle, Mary my dreams are always the most vivid after I visit there. I feel Vivian's presence the strongest on that piece of land. When is the last time you were at the castle?" Mary furrows her eyebrows.

198

"Well it's been years, I haven't been there since before I was married, before Declan was born at least."

I state firmly. "We need to go to the castle, we need to be on the grounds." We both look to each other at the same time as it dawns on us. "The vegetable garden," we speak in unison, that is where we both have seen Vivian the happiest, felt her presence the strongest. Yes, we will go to the garden.

Chapter 21

We need to deal with the present before we conjure up the past. We begin with Declan. Luckily, he is resting comfortably with numerous fractures and broken bones, in one of the stately guest rooms. Grandma and Anna will be around if anything comes up. My mother is busy packing up and last minute shopping. My father is finishing his project at work. A quick phone call to ask if I can hang out at the manor house, for one more day is a relief for the both of them. They can finish their work in peace. I give a promise I will stop by later for fresh clothes.

After an almost hot shower with the old manor house pipes grumbling, I stand in front of the mirror to gather my strength. The roar that was my headache is now a dulling thud. The wound on my chest has healed a little. The red rim that outlined the cut is now fading into more of a peachy pink. Taking a deep breath and a long once over at the image looking back, I say aloud. "Lets do this thing." The girl looking back appears far more confident than I feel.

A huge breakfast pleases Grandma, and grosses me out. We head up to the castle. Anna is so engrossed in the new puppy she decides she will stay back. Since we aren't sure how long it will take, we decide it is probably best to drive. We carry no supplies. That is until Mary steps away, pulling open an archaic door attached to a garage, she returns moments later with sacks.

We smile a reassuring nod as she throws them in the back seat. Both of us know what we need to do with those. After a tense minute of silence, I ask Mary in my stuffiest fake accent; "I mean really, what does one bring to conjure up a ghost?" This brings only an awkward half laugh and a silence equally strange. Mary slows the car before we reach the top, stopping in the middle of the long road leading to the castle. Taking a deep breath she buries her head down trying to almost disappear into the steering wheel. I again try to fumble for something to say. "I know this is hard, but we have to go. We have to try." She takes a moment before raising her head. " You must think I am a silly fool, Audrey. It is just that it has taken years to try to erase all these dreams, and now the thought that we are going to try to bring them back. Well, it just seems really odd, that's all." Now it's my turn for a tense laugh. "Believe me, these dreams, the seals, everything about this summer has been beyond odd for me, a real trip."

The rest of the ride and the walk to the castle ruins are in silence. We each play nervously with the old sacks Mary has brought. We ask simultaneously, "What now?" Followed with another awkward half laugh. We decide to sit down and talk about what we remember doing in the dream, when we are here. This is definitely a place where Vivian seems the happiest and the most peaceful.

"Maybe if we try working the garden or what we do when we are here with her? She loves picking the fresh fruit and vegetables." Mary reminds me that there hasn't been fruit or vegetables up here for years, probably centuries.

I add," The only other thing I can think of is the seaweed." Mary's face brightens. "Yes, seaweed, I have lugged many a sack full up the trail. Vivian puts it on her garden. "My first thought is lug it up, like from the ocean?" Looking out at where the land drops. "Mary, you mean you want to carry it up, not bring it in the car?"

Mary begins walking, no, more like running, towards the cliff's edge. "Here, look the trail, come along. We can climb down. It looks like the path is still there. We can do it." Peering over the edge sends a dizzy queasiness from my stomach and moves throughout my body, giving me a sort of numb feeling. Directly below us where the tall grass stops and the sheer rock face begins, lays a straight drop down to the ocean. Somewhere just before the death drop, there is a small zigzag of a shadow that probably served at one time as a trail.

She pulls at my arm as she starts down. " Oh come on, its no bother." There is that dreaded no bother again. "No bother, the last time your niece told me something was no bother, I had a nettle sting. That was a real bother. So no offense but nothing scares me more than when you guys say, no bother."

To say the path is treacherous is an under statement. Every step causes tiny rocks and dirt to start rolling and falling. My feet slide out a number of times. Mary seems completely at ease, her feet mechanically gripping with each step. The breeze and the view are incredible. I can see the entire harbor and village, as well as far out to sea.

The path opens onto a patch of white beach. It is an oasis completely hidden from view by huge dark rocks and cliffs. The sand is thick and heavy under our feet. We wander around admiring all the caves and inlets. "Mary, this is amazing, does anyone even know about this place?" Mary sighs, we both sink down in the lush sand, rich and untamed, completely untouched by humans. She looks scared as she says. "That's just it, I don't know anything about this place. I have never been here before, that's the bizarre thing. I mean I have been here in my dreams with Vivian. I don't know Audrey, I am afraid to bring all this up again. It really took a toll on me. I don't think we should be fooling in this dream stuff. We should let things be. The past is over, what is done is done." As she speaks she scoops handfuls of sand and lets it run through her hands that are cupped. The sand runs through her fingers like an hourglass.

"This is different now, before you thought it was all in your head. You were alone and frightened by these dreams, now you have me. I have them too. This isn't something inside of your head, your mind didn't invent this, it happened. It isn't like we went looking for this. Remember, Vivian came to us. She needs our help. We have to at least try. We owe it to her. I am in this thing, and if you don't help, I am going through with it anyway. One way or another."

Mary smiles as she pulls herself up brushing sand away. She lowers an arm. "Fearless Freya, nothing ever seems to scare you." She pulls me up before adding. "Alright then, lets go."

We begin gathering up piles of seaweed, long tentacles of dark green weeds that have been drying in the sun. A layer of dusty salt brushes off onto our hands and clothing. We decide to make a couple of piles and then we take the longest pieces and bind them together. After that we will load them into the sacks. Then climb back up the path. The salt dust flakes up and into my nostrils, which starts me coughing, which starts my headache all over again. Mary walks over a look of concern crosses her face. "Look, that's plenty, lets rest a bit before we start back up." She guides me into a large tuft of sand and takes off her wind jacket, and lays it on the sand. She gestures for me. I sit down and lean slightly back. I hadn't realized how tired I was.

The warmth of the hearth flushes my face, as I lean in ladling the watery broth into the small wooden bowl. The small child sits cross - legged, her tiny body so frail. Her skin so pale and her sunken eyes stare at me listlessly. I try to place the ladle in her hand, but she is too weak. She looks so frail and pathetic. Wearing an old feedbag that Vivian has cut to fit over her head makes her appear even more wretched.

A small bit of rope tied around her tiny waist is all we could muster up; we had nothing else to fit such a little frame. Slowly, I coax her to take another sip. After a few small drinks she takes more. Her stomach is in the habit of being hungry, so now it rejects the watery gruel. I am afraid to give her any of the vegetables, or a bite off the large hunk of animal lard in her weakened state. Just as I feared, she begins gagging. " Slow, here just take a small bit, there is a good girl, we will have you back eating solid food by supper, I promise." I speak as soft and gentle as I can. It takes nothing to frighten her away into her silent retreat.

She sits for hours staring at the fire rocking, almost catatonic. She seems to understand what I am saying, but is unable or unwilling to answer. Rummaging around the room with my eyes, I spy an old sewing box, small bits of colored fabric, peaking out. I take a seat next to her trying to make the odds and ends into anything that might amuse her, if even for a second.

I fashion a small head stuffed with rags, then a sack dress over top similar to the one she wears. I poke around the fire finding a coal that is relatively cool. I pick it up and draw a small face. Grabbing a bunch of twine, I easily fashion it into an upbraided hairstyle. She pretends not to be watching, but I can tell she is. It is crude and a little charming, a bit like us I guess.

Slowly, I dance the small stuffed creature around in front of her, humming a little ditty and moving her tiny head. The girl lets out a small giggle, sounds more like a guttural choke, but it is followed by a slight smile. I hand her the doll. She clutches it tightly, burying it in to her small chest. Cleaning up, I watch proudly as she begins to play with the doll. She copies the way I made the little creature dance. "We will have to find a name for her, I reckon." She looks back at me, her mouth begins to try to form words, " Paaa...Paa... olly..." or something like that comes out. "Polly, did ye say Polly." She lets off another smile; a slight recollection crosses her face. I know better than to push for more about her past. Letting my questions go for now I add as casually as I can, "Polly, that is a fine name for the little lass. I love it." With that she gives the homemade doll a proud look and a tight hug. Well I'll be, there may be a way to reach that poor little creature after all.

My feet are slightly chilled and damp. I wake to the tide slowly rolling in. It is still a ways out, but the mist from the lapping sea is splashing a wet vapor at our feet. Mary sits next to me her arms stretched over her legs, elbows resting on knees, her head cradled inside. Afraid to wake her in case she is asleep, I look out towards the village, a glare keeps glinting back at me. The sun catching on something metal sends a glint out across the channel and into our little lagoon. Like someone sending a message with a shiny mirror. It takes only a minute for me to register what I am looking at. A second more to know what it is that I need to do, with this information.

Mary hears the raven. She looks up as it circles overhead. It is my turn to help her out of the sand. I grab her hand and give a pull as I ask. "Did you have a rest?" both of us know what my real question is, did you have any dreams? "I haven't napped like that in years." Is all she needs to say, I nod. I point to the grates. "I can get into the village through the grates. I know the way. I will find the blacksmith before he leaves for the castle.

Looking over my shoulder, Mary points towards the woods. " The few survivors who tried to save loved ones from being sold to the slave ships. The people on the small boats that survived the soldiers marauding arrows, traveled that way into the woods. They camp in there for a few nights before they flee. Those poor people made a feeble attempt to chase down the boats. There loved ones are taken and then they were banished from returning to the village. I will start with them. I will head in that direction." She points over to a small wooded out-cropping. She continues in a brave tone, " I will round up as many as I can before they leave, and bring them up to Vivian's castle. Whoever arrives at the castle first must prepare Vivian for visitors, she must not freak out."

I smile at the thought before adding. "She doesn't always have the best social skills, if you know what I mean." We both know that the only way this will work is if we can get everyone to work together. Otherwise we are doomed. We quietly tie the bags filled with long leaves of seaweed to our backs, and begin the treacherous hike back up to the castle. Mary lets me go first, that way she can steady me if and when I begin to falter on the trail. We walk quietly for a while, both silently planning our trip.

The doubt and fear of the trip that lies ahead of me supersedes any fear I have of the cliff I am presently climbing. Neither one of us want to say the obvious fear that is in both our heads. As we climb off the path and into the huge meadow that leads to the kitchen garden.

Mary turns to me. "We will need to take our time laying the seaweed in the garden. We must show great patience, and even greater concentration on the tasks we need to accomplish, later in our dreams." It is my turn to feel insecure. I grab her arm and stop her. "Mary, what if we don't go back to where we want to tonight, how can we possibly make this work?" I am almost paralyzed by anxiety now. She shakes her head,

"I know, I know," she says in a whisper. "You don't think I have the same doubts as you do? It was your brave words that have gotten me this far. Remember what you said. We have to try. We owe Vivian at least a try."

We quietly and gracefully untie the seaweed from each other's backs. We make two piles and begin laying it on top of what once was a bountiful garden. Neatly we pack the area tight with the large strands. We fertilize and prepare the ground as if underneath lies a harvest. Ignoring what is here now, which is an unruly, unkempt, cow pasture. When stones from the castle block the way, neatly we put them back and pile them up where we think the main structure once stood. All the while one single raven flies over our head circling, tighter and tighter - sometimes a quiet chatter, other times she lets out a scream.

Chapter 22

The evening at the manor passes quietly. Mary and I act happy and engaging. If only one thing can be said about our behavior tonight, it is that we are acting boring and normal. I would never imagine it would take so much out of us to pretend. It seems so blatantly obvious our minds are elsewhere. Anna shows us all the progress she has made with her puppy, which is almost a lot. He can almost sit, he can almost come, and he is pretty close to being housebroken. I say this as I run to get the towel paper and some rug cleaner.

Grandma's face drops in disappointment as she says, "it is eight thirty, what do you mean you're all going to bed, what about the chat shows? Who is going to watch them with me?" Even Anna is worn out. Mary helps Declan climb the last of the steps and head towards his bedroom. He has made an incredible recovery, but still tires easily.

Climbing into bed, I am physically exhausted. After a few minutes, I realize I am not at all mentally tired. In fact my mind is racing. I go back to the trip under the tunnels to save the seals. I retrace each step being careful to only stay in the old aqueducts, in my memories. I think about the smell and the feel of the old tunnels, that grungy disgusting sludgy water. The thickness of the mud on my feet as I wade through.

It is freezing, I shiver, the water so deep and cold. The smell is so acrid and pungent. Echoing off the dingy wall I hear a squeak from another occupant. I let out a scream, its rats. There are rats in the water, rats on the ledges, rat's overhead dropping into the grates.

Above me a bustling crowded village. Mud and horse manure drop down from every opening in the grates. I move through trying to find a quiet space, it seems so packed, how will I slip in? I can't just climb out from the sewers.

Moving along looking up at every sunlit opening. Finally, a grate above that is quiet and dark. I shimmy up the side of the wet stone, grabbing the grate and locking my fingers over the top. I pull myself up with all my weight. The grate moves, it is not attached at all but just lies loose. I use all my strength to get far enough to look. It seems to be just under an overhang, the street is quiet. I push the grate, but it remains stuck in the small cobblestone groove its been fitted into. It gives a wiggle.

The way I am positioned makes it awkward for me to hold my body up and move the grate. No matter how much I will it, it remains impossible to open. Straining to hold on, I hear a whistle far off at first, now closer. A small boy with a dirty face steps above just missing my finger. "Excuse me kind sir, could I bother you for a small favor?" The boy stops but doesn't look down. "Here, down here, could you help me, I seem to be stuck down in the grate. Would you mind helping me to lift the iron, please?"

He bends down a look of complete shock on his face, "I say missy, what'cha doing down there?" "I umm seem to have dropped a coin, and when I bent to pick it up, I slipped, and well the next thing I knew I was stuck." He stops to think about it for a minute, and then starts to pull the grate off, "Wait a minute. If that is the case, then how did the grate get back on?"

I take only a minute before I say, " Uhh, I think when I was leaning in I may have accidently hit it back into place." He begins to back up a little skeptical. "Oh please, I need your help." This stops him for a minute, " What would it be worth to you?" I look down, at my soiled dress. "My pockets are empty, I have nothing to give. Please can't you just help me?" He thinks for a minute or two and then says, "I'd be needing to deliver this wood, if you would agree to help, I might be able to get you out. Otherwise, I am sure the guards will be by, and they would be only to eager to help you."

As I straighten up, and brush the sewer sludge off, I see his small wobbly cart is over - flowing with wood. It takes only a few steps to understand what his idea of helping is. I pull the wagon, unloading all the heavy wood. He walks alongside whistling that same horrible tune over and over. It takes most of my strength just to pull the wooden wheels along the old cobblestone. We are moving so slowly with the weight of the wagon, it is easy to catch sight of the old woman following.

In fact, if I recall she has been following us for most of the way, walking at an incredibly slow pace, even for a woman of her age. When I catch her eye she looks down, or pretends to be looking the other direction. I barely whisper to the boy, " I need to find the blacksmith. It is really important I find him. I have helped with nearly all the wood." He points to the open market, "Oisin's barn is on the other side of the market, you may bring the rest of the wood there and leave the wagon. It belongs to him anyway, I kind of borrowed it."

I quickly cross the road, hoping to shake the woman in the crowd in the market. "Oisin are you here?" I drop the wagon and look around the barn, circling the amulets, the only occupant, a young man, stands with his head down. "Have you seen Oisin, the blacksmith, I must find him?" The boy looks me over once. "He isn't here and he won't be here today." I speak over him. "I must find him, I have information about his daughter." The boy steps up. "What do you know about my sister?"

"I know where she is, he must come with me. The guards took her. I know where she is." The boy takes a step backward, a look of fear crosses over his face. I step in closer to tell him, he must hurry.

Suddenly my feet are lifted off the ground. "Well what have we here, a little sewer rat, caught scurrying through town." The grip the stranger has on my shoulder is so tight. A huge hand holds me by my shoulder blade bone. My hair is being pulled out along with my collarbone. A soldier stands on each side. "What do you know of this girl?" A bellowing question to the young man sends him pulling back in fear. "Nothing, I don't know anything about her, she came asking for the blacksmith, that is all." They begin dragging me away, I call back over my shoulder, " He needs to come and you must tell him, I know where she is. Her only words are about Polly."

We round the corner onto a back alley, the old woman scampers behind us. "That is her, that is the one who crawled out of the sewer. Remember you promised me a coin." With that, one of the soldiers pulls a coin and tosses it on the muddy ground. The old woman bends down to pick it up. The soldier kicks her and she falls down. "Now mind yourself, old woman."

"We should be able to get a nice bit of gold for this one, aye." They both begin to look me over. The cough rattles deep in my belly. I can't stop myself. I fall into a coughing fit. Dropping me, I collapse in a heap at their feet. "You best not have the plague, wench." The guard adds while he kicks me in the stomach. " I say we throw her in the dungeon, and if she lives through the night, we sell her tomorrow eve."

The larger of the two bends to pick me up, the force to the back of his head comes so fast and hard. I am startled when he falls on top of me. His companion drops with a blow to the stomach. He tries to stand when he is punched in the face. Out cold, both, one is on top of me in a heap, the other rests at my feet. I push the heavy weight of the unconscious guard off me. Standing over me a stocky man, dressed in black. He looks down at me before he yells. "Where is she? Where is my Aine? I scramble to get up before responding. "She is safe. She is at the castle." My voice answers hoarsely from all the coughing. His voice becomes skeptical. "What castle do you speak of?"

Slowly standing up, I watch the old woman slinking around the corner. "Oisin, I am glad I could help, would you still be wiling to give me that bit of silver we spoke of?"

He turns around a look of anger mixes with the skepticism on his face. "If this is some plan you two have cooked up to get some money out me, so help me I will kill you both with me bare hands."

Once the woman has the coin she begins to fall back in the shadows. I speak cautiously. "We must leave right away. We must get out of the village, that woman will sell any information she can, she must not hear what I am to say."

We turn the corner in time to see a large wagon headed directly at us. I try to give the information about his daughter as quickly as I can." Your daughter was on a boat in the harbor, the soldiers were going to sell her to the slave ships. Vivian rescued her, along with a few others. Some died, but your daughter, she lives.

She is at the castle now she is injured but alive. She seems shaken..." I pause before adding sadly. "Well, she doesn't really speak." Oisin smiles. "It is Aine, thank God she is safe, please you must take me to her."

The young man at the blacksmith shop earlier is driving the old cart pulled by two huge draft horses. Barreling full speed at us. "What did you bring, son?" The man asks, throwing me into the back. "I grabbed what I could, we were already stocked to travel out to fix the shoes on the horses in the huntsman party." He pauses, " and I grabbed this." With that he holds up a tiny doll. "Polly" I add. The man turns to me. "You best be telling the truth, once we head out those gates, there will be no coming back." He climbs onto the over - loaded carriage and grabs the reins from his son.

"Now get down under the blankets, stay quiet. Don't come out at all, if you want to make it out of this village. Oh and take this," his huge hand clumsily passes me the doll.

A stained blanket is thrown over me. I subdue a cough as best I can, but my sickness and the stench off the old blanket is wretched. The wagon lurches ahead, traveling far too fast for the narrow cobblestone roads. The horse's hooves slide on the stones as they try to dig in for traction. We are racing along through the city streets. I hear people hurrying to get out of the way. We stop, I hear Oisin speak. "Open the gates, quickly." A voice from overhead, coming from the guard tower yells. "What is your hurry, blacksmith?" There is a pause before the voice yells again. "Why do you speak to me so disrespectfully?" " I am sorry sir, it is just that the huntsman's horse has thrown a shoe, and they are on the trail of a great stag. I have been beckoned to come immediately." Oisin's voice although pleading, doesn't reveal his lie.

There is a silence. The guardsman waits, before he bellows. "Open the gate, allow the blacksmith through." The sound of many feet, then a huge rattling of wood and metal scraping, follows a creaking sound as it opens. The ground shakes with the weight of each door being moved. We begin to move through, a voice faint in the background, a man yelling. His voice grows louder with his approach. "Shut the gate, don't let them pass, STOP THAT WAGON."

There is the sound of a scuffle. The wagon squeezes
through. A grotesque creaking sound as wood splinters
off the sides of our wagon. We can barely make it
through the opening of the gates. Oisin is prompting the
horses to go forward. We are almost out.

The wagon sags under the weight of a person
jumping on. The old tarp lifts. A soldier with yellow
teeth leans in. His stale breath blows in my face. He
lets out a delighted victory cry. "Awee," that is all he
says before I hear a thud, something large has hit him
in the back of the head. The blacksmith's son pushes
him off the wagon. Oisin standing, with his back to me

commands the horse. The reins buckle as he smacks them down, the leather slapping the flesh of the menacing beasts. Oisin lets out a roar. "Get, Yah." The wagon lurches again. The powerful draft horses hooves land on the soft earth and dig in. It is like we take flight. The wheels on the wagon feel as if they will spiral and fly off. We are traveling so fast. Mud from the mighty hooves fly up and splatter us. The pace is such that I grow dizzy as my cough begins again.

Oisin reins the horses, "WHOAAA" he slows to a walk. He turns the rig and heads down a path, winding along the water's edge, heading back towards the village. "What are you doing? We can't go back." My voice is a desperate shrill. "We won't get far with this load, the woods will be filled with soldiers, they will over - take us in no time. We must lighten our load. You and Tomas will travel by sea. I will take the horses and the empty wagon." Oisin looks to the sky. "It will be dark soon enough, if I can confuse the soldiers long enough they will give up and camp. They will never go up to the castle, its got the…" Oisin pauses and then looks me over. "The villagers all think its evil ground, its covered in the black death." No one will step foot up there. We will load the boat; you two stay close to the water's edge, just out of sight. I can meet you over there." He says pointing to the woods edge.

"I can get us into the castle by water. I know of a cave that leads to the interior of the castle." I tell him. I am proud I can contribute something to this mission.

Piles of seaweed and rotted wood litter the waters edge. Oisin walks confidently up to a pile of debris that looks exactly like all the others; he pulls back the tangle of weeds to expose a small wood boat, with a number of crude oars.

We spend the rest of the early evening unloading the blacksmith's tools onto the boat. Oisin and Tomas have the strength of four men. We sometimes hear the sounds of the gates opening and groups of riders leaving. They gallop off into the woods in small parties. Each group of soldiers and their horses erase any evidence of our tracks. Not one of the soldiers ever considering that we would have double backed.

We climb onto the boat. Oisin pushes us into the dark calm sea. " I will see you both in a day or two at the castle. The fog is rolling in, it will give us all cover." The blacksmith grabs his son's arm. "Son, no matter what, keep your sister safe. Make sure you mind the tools and the boat, they are all we have to start over again." Tomas leans over and gives his father a hug. "Yes Father, be careful."

Our boat glides off silently in the darkness. The weight of the tools leaves us heavy in the water, steadying us against the waves. Tomas uses all his strength to guide us along. It is pitch black in the lagoon. The only sound is the slight whoosh of our boat as it slowly cuts a path across the basin. Each time I try to help to paddle I am sent into a coughing jag. Tomas finally says, "Try to rest for a while, I will need you to show me the cave in a few hours."

It is so dark I can't see his face, making it easier to ask what has been nagging at me since I have met these two gentlemen. "Why are you not afraid of me, you know I carry the sickness?"

The paddle laps the water a few more times before he responds. "My mother, she died from the sickness. My father and sister and me, we didn't catch it." Tomas goes on to explain that is why they are here in this village. They had to flee from their last place when the locals found about his mother being sick.

That makes sense to me now. I understand why Oisin is so obsessed with bringing the tools. It is the reason he was allowed to enter the walled village. He is an amazing blacksmith and horseman. He has done business with Vivian. He isn't afraid of her giving him the black death because he knows is immune.

Tomas goes on to tell me about Aine, his sister. She spoke before their mother got sick but when she died, she pretty much stopped communicating at all. Except to that doll. Aine went everywhere with that doll, it was the last thing her mother made for her. It became her whole life.

Tomas speaks about how they knew Aine was taken. She would never wander off without bringing her beloved Polly. That is also why his father knew I was telling the truth.

Paddling in silence, I wonder if I should tell Tomas about my mother, possibly prepare him for what to expect. Tomas fills the silence with the last of his stories. "We knew you were telling the truth Freya when you mentioned the doll. When you said she barely spoke, we were convinced. My father decided we would give you a chance. If you were lying, or had done something to Aine, he said we would kill you on the spot."

I shiver and pull the smelly tarp up around my shoulders. Judging from how capable these two have been so far at our escape. I have no doubt that killing me would be absolutely no bother for them.

In between coughs Tomas fills me with stories of his family, how gallant his father is, and wonderful his mother was. I imagine they had a wonderful life before the sickness game.

His father has had dealings with Vivian and is familiar with some of her habits. Oisin told Tomas he has traded with Vivian, and she was always fair and decent. He doesn't think Vivian is possessed by the devil or insane. He thinks Vivian has been a victim of many horrible events that have scarred her. Oisin told his son he thought somewhere inside Vivian there was a kind person.

Finding the opening to the cave proves far more treacherous then I imagined. I am fading in and out of consciousness; the pain in my head grows more intense. I am not even sure if Tomas or maybe it was me is the one who spots the dark crevice that leads to the cave. I do remember the sound of wings. The ravens, aware that I am on the boat lead the craft through the dark channels. We see the torches burning in the distance and the figure of Vivian stands ready at the pier. She seems to be expecting us. The air becomes much warmer as we enter, no longer feeling the sea breeze that has frozen me to the bone. She stands with her hands clasped the large emerald necklace around her neck catching the torches reflection.

I awake in the manor house. I can tell it is the middle of the night because it is quiet and dark. I start to sit up, but my pounding headache sends me lying back down. My hair is wet and sticky against my face. I pull the covers up close around my chin. I am so cold, so very cold. I can hear the creak and rumbles of the old house. I cry out. My throat is so dry. I can't form the words.

Aine's soft voice is singing in my ear. She pulls me back to the castle. "Achoo, achoo we all fall down", as she sings she dances her pretty little doll Polly around by its petite arms, the dolls dress puffs in and out with each bar of the song. Vivian smiles down at me, pushing my hair back. I can see a small tear spill over her overflowing eyes and roll down her cheek. I try to speak, to sit up, but I am frozen. My body lays in position ready to pass on.

I smell flowers, lovely flowers. Vivian delicately lifts my hand. She places a beautiful ring on my finger and a small bouquet in my hands. Neatly she folds my hands around them. Standing behind her are Tomas, and Oisin. Is that Catherine coming over? I look out the window to a beautiful day. I hear the ravens scream. Why is everyone crying?

I wake up back in the old manor house. Mary is crying. "Are you okay, I ask?" She nods, "I am better than I have ever been Audrey, thank you." She runs a hand over my forehead before adding with a small bit of sadness. "We did it." A calm peace settles over me, my headache is gone and my fever has broken.

My voice shakes slightly as I speak. "Mary, we saved more than just Vivian. We saved Aine, and her family, hopefully countless others. I sit up and look out the long window. It looks like a beautiful day."

Chapter 23

My father yells upstairs. "Audrey, come on down." I finish stuffing the last of my things out of the funny shaped closet and into my striped suitcase. I take a final look around the room. Turning off the light I make my way down the many small staircases.

Anna hugs me tight, as Bear finds a quiet place on the carpet to do his business. She fills me in on all the exciting plans. Declan and Mary are going to fix the manor house up to make a Bed and Breakfast. Meanwhile Granny can stay in this house with Anna, her Mom, and Bear, she is so excited.

Deidre and Dad are busy discussing more business for the coming year. They make plans for next summer's assignment.

Mom lets the rest of the crew in. Granny gives me a hug. My mother thanks her for letting me stay at her house. "Well, the child is no bother, goodness gracious, she does sleep a lot." My mother nods with a confused expression on her face.

Declan gives me an awkward half hug, his oversized cast makes it cumbersome and difficult to hug him back. Anna runs in between us, " I can't wait for you to come next year, we can go down to the caves. Rumor has it, some boys got trapped down there, and now their ghosts..." she is so excited to tell me the story. I stop her mid-sentence. "Maybe next year, I have had enough excitement for one summer." Declan and Anna nod thinking of our seal adventure. Mary puts her hand on my shoulder. Brian steps behind me and says, "Jack, can I have a moment of your time? There is something I need to go over with you."

Mary, and I embrace in a knowing hug. "Can I see you for a moment outside luv? "We step out past the piano, and onto the back deck. The horses are grazing in the warm sun. They give only a slight look up at this mild intrusion, and then continue eating the rich velvet grass. Mary fumbles around in her pocket before looking at me. She starts to say something, but stops herself. I smile at her.

Pulling my hand, she extends my fingers, slowly gracefully, with the same care as Vivian; she places the ring back on my finger. I recognize it immediately. The huge emerald stone is surrounded by diamonds, "I can't take this. It is worth a fortune." Mary stops me, "It doesn't belong to me, Audrey. I was merely holding on to it for you." Brian is going over the paperwork with your father right now. It is yours. I am left speechless.

We pull to the end of the driveway; the young Kennedy boy is just wrapping up the last of the red ribbon. The road we are about to turn on to is covered in cows. "We will have to go the other way." My dad says. Slightly agitated, as he swings the car around.

The car climbs the hill. " Wow, someone is sure having a party, look at all those lights at the top. I didn't know anyone lived up there, behind the woods. I thought it was just a cow pasture?" Before I can answer my father, I look up.

She must have a lantern on in every window of that castle. I remember how long that would have taken. I raise my hand. The last of the evening sun mixed with a strange glow filters through the ring on my finger, sending shimmery green gold warmth through the car.

I look through the many cut facets of the stone, through the golden haze. In my field of vision inside the ring held up to the window is a magnificent castle completely intact and spectacular. It is thriving and alive with movement and people. Flowers bloom and towers stand tall where once there was ruin, sadness and decay.

"Good bye, I will miss you." I whisper. A raven far above our heads lets out a last call.

ACKNOWLEDGMENTS

Many thanks to many people, listed below are just a few:

To my sisters, brother, mother, and husband for all the love and support throughout the process. Fergus O'Connell for his valuable advice. Darin Jewell for his patience, wisdom and experience. Jonah Levy for his meticulous and talented editing. Diane Minsker and all the media center directors and workers for their dedication to bringing great reads to fresh minds. Olivia Clinton for starting me on the adventure. Gabriel Gruttadaro for walking with me every step of the way.